SINCE

YOU

WENT

AWAY

SINCE YOU

WENT AWAY

Part One: Winter

Nan
McCarthy

RAINWATER
PRESS

Since You Went Away by Nan McCarthy

Part One: Winter

Rainwater Press

www.nan-mccarthy.com

Cover design by David J. High, highdzn.com
Interior design by Kevin Callahan, BNGObooks.com + David J. High
Cover art from a painting by Larry Jacobsen, © Can Stock Photo / DesignWest
Author photo by Kelly Anderson Cole

Published in the United States of America by Rainwater Press.
For information please use the contact form on the author's website
www.nan-mccarthy.com/contact/.

ISBN 978-1-888354-12-6 (paperback)

ISBN 978-1-888354-16-4 (ebook)

Third Edition: March 2019

for Pat, Ben & Coleman

Contents

Characters & Places

Liam Mahoney Emilie's husband, Finn & Rory's dad, colonel, U.S. Marine Corps

Emilie Mahoney Liam's wife, Finn & Rory's mom, high school In-School Suspension supervisor

Finn Mahoney senior in high school/freshman in college, Liam & Emilie's older son

Rory Mahoney freshman/sophomore in high school, Liam & Emilie's younger son

Soda Mahoney family long-haired Chihuahua mix (rescue)

Brig Mahoney family Highland Terrier mix (rescue)

Smedley Mahoney family cat, gray long-hair mix (rescue)

Button Mahoney family cat, calico mix (rescue)

Daly Mahoney family cat, tan short-hair mix (rescue)

Ozzy Rory's bearded dragon lizard

Elvis Rory's goldfish

Ahmad Iraqi interpreter living in U.S., friend of Fakhir and DeYoungs

Fakhir al-Azzawi Iraqi interpreter living in U.S., friend of Wade, Liam, and Ray

Farah al-Azzawi Fakhir's youngest sister

Arifa al-Azzawi Fakhir's mom

DeYoungs Marine Corps family hosting Ahmad

Ray Salazar works with Liam, husband of Janet, major, U.S. Marine Corps, original hosts of Fakhir

Janet Salazar wife of Ray, friend of Emilie, original hosts of Fakhir

Agnes Hawkins neighbor, wife of Eugene, mother of Ethan, book club member

Eugene Hawkins neighbor, husband of Agnes, father of Ethan

Ethan Hawkins neighbor, son of Agnes & Eugene Hawkins, friend of Rory

Crystal Finn's date to Turnabout dance, friend, bandmate

Ashley Rory's date to Turnabout dance

Wanda Reszel neighbor, wife of Vince, friend of Emilie, book club member

Vince Reszel neighbor, husband of Wanda

Wade Miller family friend of Liam & Emilie, friend of Fakhir, major (ret.), U.S. Marine Corps

Isabel Miller Wade's 2nd (& current) wife

Chloe Miller Wade & Isabel's baby girl

Shelley Wade's 1st wife

Rourke Mahoney Liam's dad, retired Marine, Korean War veteran, deceased

Mary Mahoney Liam's mom

Lucia Caputo ISS student

Raquel Caputo Lucia's mom

Carmen Caputo Lucia's dad

Andy, Arthur, Angel Caputo Lucia's three younger brothers

Mr. Lavin Finn's piano teacher

Ken Phillips fellow colonel who works with Liam, husband of Tammy

Tammy Phillips Col. Phillips' wife, friend of Emilie, eventual book club member

Tiffany Emilie's coworker who asks annoying questions about Liam's deployment

Neil Harris Finn's high school friend and bandmate

Suzanne & Mike Harris Neil's parents

Darryl Finn's high school friend and bandmate

Josh Rory's friend, lives in neighborhood

Aunt Dottie Emilie's aunt (sister of Emilie's deceased mother)

Joey Aunt Dottie's boyfriend

Wally Aunt Dottie's 1st husband, deceased

Jacques Aunt Dottie's Jack Russell terrier

Bonnie Aunt Dottie's next-door neighbor who petsits Jacques

Marcus ISS student

Derek ISS student

Chancee Bunco hostess

Pamela lives in the neighborhood

Dr. Hermey Mahoney family dentist

Genie book club member

Patty   book club member

Barb   book club member

Roxanne   book club member

Kim   book club member

Charlene   book club member

Dr. Gouwens   principal at Finn & Rory's high school, Emilie's boss

Portia   yoga instructor

Coach Crowley   Rory's track coach

Mrs. Callahan   Lucia's Language Arts teacher

Mrs. Schaeffer   Lucia's History teacher

Mr. Zim (Zimmerman)   Finn & Lucia's Nutrition teacher

Brian   Lucia's boyfriend

Officer Dempsey   High School Resource Officer

Mrs. Nelson   assistant principal at the high school

Gerald Lewis   Liam's commanding officer, brigadier general, U.S. Marine Corps

Virginia Lewis   wife of BGen. Lewis, facilitator of FSG (Family Support Group)

Jerri Jablonski   wife of Maj. Jablonski, head of FSG

Maj. Jablonski   husband of Jerri, Liam's coworker

LtCol. Dobson (Ret.)   director of MWR (Morale, Welfare, & Recreation)

"Mrs. Baez" (alias)   spouse at FSG meeting

"Mr. Baez" (alias)   service member who works in Liam's shop and is married to "Mrs. Baez"

Leah Gibson previously known as "Mrs. Baez," friend of Emilie, book club member

Jacob Gibson previously known as "Mr. Baez," Leah's husband, corporal, U.S. Marine Corps

Frank ISS student

Ronny head custodian at the high school

Colin Liam's youngest brother

Kurt Rory's friend

Billy Rory's friend

GySgt. Lee retired gunnery sergeant (U.S. Marine Corps) at American Legion

Officer Andrews police officer in Buell City Police Department

John Emilie's brother

Stevens family neighbors who live behind Mahoneys

Greg Wade's 2nd counselor at the VA

Francis Emilie's step-father, deceased

Mel Finn's college roommate

Riikka Girl from Finland who plays on Rory's hockey team

Fiona Liam and Emily's niece

SSgt. Scott Marine recruiter

Buell City fictional Midwest town where Mahoney family lives

Fidelia's coffee shop where Finn works

Mondo fictional company that sells things on the Internet

Peroni's pizza place near Mahoney house

Smollett's ice cream parlor near Mahoney house

Wakeville fictional Midwest town three hours from Buell City & the site of a Mondo fulfillment center.

Part One

Winter

A note from the author:

*A glossary on page 127 explains
military terms & acronyms used in this story.*

Of all the times we've had to say goodbye, today was the hardest. Twenty-five years of goodbyes. You'd think it would get easier over time but it doesn't. Two months in Korea, three months in Colombia, four months in Beirut, five months in Afghanistan, six months in Iraq. Now, your second time to Iraq, and the longest deployment yet. Twelve months. Winter, spring, summer, fall. Four seasons without you.

When the boys were little I could pop them in the car and take them to the zoo, or the beach, or the movies — anywhere, really — and I was somehow able to mend the hole in their hearts each time you went away. Now, it's harder. They're teenagers. They've been through a lot, and they know too much. Will I be enough for them?

By the time you pulled us in for one final embrace as we stood outside security, I felt as if I were watching the scene unfold from a distance. It was too painful to be inside my own body. I'm sorry if I seemed unemotional. The truth is, it was all I could do to hold myself together in front of Finn and Rory. I wanted to be strong — for them and for you — and I knew if I let one teardrop fall I'd come completely undone. So when we watched you walk away through the terminal doors, I held everything inside as best I could — knowing we all were doing the same.

On the drive back home, the boys and I let the sadness settle over us. After the strain and apprehension of the past month, at least now we no longer had to dread the moment of goodbye. It was finally over, and we could get on with the business of living life without you. Was it the same for you, once you passed through the gate and settled into your seat on the plane?

When we walked in the house, everything looked different knowing you wouldn't be back soon. Your half-empty coffee cup on the kitchen counter, the photo on the fridge of the four of us in Hawaii, your car keys in the wooden bowl where you drop them every night along with your loose change and the pocketknife from your dad.

Upstairs, I slipped off my shoes and wrapped myself in your bathrobe. Your side of the bathroom where you had cleared away your toiletries looked barren. The only thing left was your wet bath towel, which you had draped over my vanity chair. (A habit of yours that drives me crazy — but now I'm going to miss.) Even your nightstand looked lonesome with your stack of books waiting to be read and the empty coaster where you set your water every night. I sat in the rocking chair your brothers gave you at your last promotion, picturing you sitting there before bed, reading a book or playing solitaire on your phone. It hurt to think of you but I made myself wallow for a good long time, hoping I could at least begin to wrap my mind around the absence of you.

It's nighttime now, and as I write this email in bed with my laptop, Finn is working at the coffee shop 'til close and Rory's downstairs doing homework. Both dogs and all three cats are on your side of the bed, trying to fill the empty space you left behind. Soda is buried under the covers as usual and Brig has laid claim to your pillow, as if you'd only just left for work in the morning. The cats are at the foot of the bed snuggled against the cold. The programmable thermostat you installed before you left is right on schedule and I can already feel the temperature dropping for the night. I covered myself with the mink blanket you brought home from Korea, hoping it would keep me warm, but I wish I had you instead.

Monday, January 14, 2008   8:43 p.m.

You know how we always joke that everything in the house waits to break down until you're on deployment? Well, this time the house couldn't even wait until we got back home after dropping you at the airport yesterday! I didn't want to worry you about it last night, which is why I didn't mention it. But now that it's been fixed, I figure it's safe to tell you about our little mishap. (Which, I'm sure, is only the first in a long line of household emergencies that await us in the coming year.)

So. After a car ride home from the airport that was downright funereal, we pulled into the driveway. I press the remote, and guess what? The garage door doesn't open.

"What the hell," I say. I'm doing that thing people do, where they think if they keep pressing the button harder and harder the remote will magically start working again. I'm waving it in front of me at various angles when Rory leans forward from the back seat and takes it from my hand.

"Mom. You're not doing it right. Let me try." He points the remote directly at the garage and, in an authoritative manner, presses the button.

"Nice try dufus," Finn says, grabbing the remote from his brother. "It's probably the batteries." He shakes the remote and bangs it against his palm a few times before pressing the button—with no results.

"Now who's the dufus?" Rory says.

"Boys." I give them a warning look and the car is temporarily silent while I think things through. It's nice and toasty in the car, and I'm loathe to step out into the elements. "Why don't you guys get out and just lift the garage door for me. That's how we did it back in the day."

Knowing better than to argue with me under the circumstances, Finn and Rory exit the vehicle and trudge through the snow to lift the garage door. Except it doesn't budge. After a few more tries, they turn to look at me as if to say, "What now?"

Exhaling deeply, I turn off the ignition, get out of the nice warm car, pull the hood of my parka over my head, and clomp up the driveway. There we are, in the freezing cold, our breath vaporizing as the three of us stand in front of the dumb broken garage door looking at one another.

I'm trying to figure out if I should laugh or cry or kick a hole in the damn door with my snow boot. The boys, meanwhile, are keeping a close eye on me, obviously wondering if this is the moment I'm going to lose my shit. Here we are not even an hour after leaving you at the airport—not even inside the house yet!—and things are already going to hell in a handbasket.

So I do what any mature 46-year-old mother of two teenage boys would do—I stomp my foot and shout at the garage door. "Son of a bitch!"

The boys regard my outburst in wary silence. I don't want to upset them, and yet it occurs to me how good it would feel, at this particular moment in time, to let rip a few more swears. I decide to give in to my urge to kick the garage door with my snow boot, and while doing so I let fly a few more choice phrases. (Something along the lines of telling the garage door to go fuck itself, along with some fuckity fuck mcfucks thrown in for good measure.)

By this time Finn and Rory are looking slightly alarmed — until that is, they notice the satisfied smile that escapes my lips along with the fourth or fifth F-bomb. At this they can't help but smile too. I try pretending I'm still pissed off but it's no good. A moment ago it felt like our world was falling apart. And now we can't stop grinning at each other.

"Here's an idea," Finn says. "How about we leave the fucking car in the fucking driveway and walk through the fucking front door?"

To which Rory replies, "That's an excellent fucking idea."

Current sitrep: all good. I met the garage door guy back at the house after work today and we now have a garage door that works. Bad news? We had to get a new motor installed — to the tune of $345. It'll put a dent in the new budget I made for us based on your combat pay, but I guess there are worse things. I couldn't help but remember that time the furnace went out in the middle of January when Finn was a baby and you had just left for Cherry Point. We didn't have the money back then to call a furnace guy so you coached me over the phone and we fixed it. How many broken furnaces, leaky water heaters, stopped-up kitchen sinks, blown transmissions, and flooded basements have we survived since then?

It must have been late when you arrived in California last night with no easy access to a phone or computer. I'm wondering how your check-in is going and if you've already begun your pre-deployment training. I'm also anxious to find out when you're heading to Iraq. I know you can't give details over the phone or email so I'm guessing we'll hear you're on your way just before you leave — or maybe even after you've arrived in the Middle East. At any rate I hope you're able to find a computer to use in the next few days to check your email. Better yet, give us a call and let us know you've arrived safely.

I didn't see any breaking stories about plane crashes on TV last night so I'm pretty sure you made it there in one piece. Sad to say I'm already watching the news 24/7, like I've been doing since your very first deployment. As if they're going to show a clip of you getting off the plane in Camp Pendleton!

Tuesday, January 15, 2008   9:08 p.m.

Thank God I've started sleeping with my cell phone — I even take it to the bathroom with me now — or I would've missed your call last night. I don't know how you manage to be so cheerful all the time. You're the one who has to be away from home for twelve months, sleep in a strange and dangerous place, eat MREs and chow hall food, and go without seeing the boys day after day. The only hint I had you were the least bit anxious before you left was seeing how many times you packed and repacked your seabag.

Sounds like they've got you pretty well snapped in, since you've already started your training. Only a couple weeks and you'll be headed for Iraq. I already don't like the feeling of not being able to pick up the phone to call you. I wish we could Skype once you're over there, but I suppose I understand why they've blocked that in some places. Guess we'll just have to satisfy ourselves with emails, letters, and the occasional phone call.

Speaking of which, did you find the letter I hid in your seabag? I knew I'd be too churned up inside to say much at the airport, and I wanted to tell you how proud I am of you and what you're doing. With your rank and the job you were in before you left, you could've easily avoided another deployment to Iraq.

Thinking back to that day we took the dogs for a walk last October, I somehow knew you were going to tell me you wanted to volunteer to go to the Middle East again. Watching the younger guys get sent overseas two, three, four times, you knew the right thing to do was to make yourself available again. It's what Marines do and it's one of the reasons I married you — for time and again choosing the difficult right over the easy wrong. Though I secretly hoped the day would never come when you'd step forward again, I knew I'd fully support you before you even asked for my blessing that day. Now if only you could've been assigned one of those three- or six-month boondoggles — but twelve months? Hell's bells!

I've already gotten used to the idea of you not being here for our 25th wedding anniversary — I can't remember the last time you were home for one of our anniversaries anyway. But it hurts my heart — and I know it hurts yours too — for you to miss Rory's first season of high school hockey and Finn's graduation in the spring. As it is now they're both being stoic since you left. Either that or they're just pretending you're away on one of your shorter trips. Which is what I find myself doing when the thought of you being gone for so long is too much to bear.

Wednesday, January 16, 2008   11:15 p.m.

Wanda invited me to her house tonight for Bunco, which was thoughtful of her since I'm not part of their regular group. But I decided to pass. One, I had a busy day at work and I'm exhausted; two, I'm not up to facing people so soon after you've left; and three, Bunco is dumb.

Or maybe I just don't get it, and I'm the one who's dumb. Because I really don't see the point in mindlessly rolling dice for three hours when all you're really there for is the artichoke dip, Pinot Grigio, and the latest neighborhood gouge on whose kid got an MIP last weekend and if whatsherface's breast implants are a double or triple D. Why not just dispense with all the table-hopping, dice-rolling, mini-pencils & scorecards, and just sit around and eat, drink, and talk? Wouldn't that be a lot more relaxing? I mean, it's not like Bunco is a game of skill or anything — unless you consider being able to count and drink at the same time a skill (which might explain why I'm no good at it).

Not to be ungrateful. I do appreciate Wanda thinking of me and I hope she's not mad at me for being a party pooper.

Work today was lively to say the least. When I arrived at my desk this morning I discovered ten students would be coming to In-School Suspension for the day, outdoing my previous record of eight. I was able to scrounge up a couple extra desks from the teachers down the hall before the first bell rang, and the rest of the day was no less exciting keeping all ten students in line and on task with their homework.

Three of them had been caught trying to cut last Friday's assembly; two were found smoking in the parking lot during lunch yesterday; and several others had a collection of unexcused absences and unserved detentions. Then there was the boy who was cited for "inappropriate use of the CPR dummy" in Health class. (Some teachers just don't have a sense of humor I guess.)

Speaking of unexcused absences, Finn advised me at dinner tonight he overslept this morning after having been up all night working on a paper. He entirely missed his first-hour class. If he keeps it up he'll find himself serving an In-School Suspension with his mom. Wouldn't that be classic.

You remember Ahmad and Fakhir, the Iraqi interpreters who were at the unit Christmas party? In fact I think you said you worked with both of them on your last tour there. Since they came to the U.S., Ahmad has been staying with the DeYoungs, and Fakhir has been staying with the Salazars. But when I ran into Janet Salazar at the commissary after work today, she said they just received orders to Twentynine Palms. And they have to be there asap. There's no way Fakhir can go with them — Janet says his security clearance for that job on base is close to getting approved.

Which got me to thinking … It would be no trouble at all to let Fakhir stay here for a while until he gets on his feet. We do have the spare bedroom in the basement, and this old place is certainly big enough for an extra person or two (or three). What do you think? I told Janet I'd check with you and get back to her. I hope you don't think I'm crazy for suggesting the idea. Who knows? Helping Fakhir could be good for all of us. I mean, having a place to stay helps him obviously, but it could also be a good experience for the boys. And with Fakhir around to take our minds off you being away, the months ahead might just go by a little faster.

Thursday, January 17, 2008   10:02 p.m.

I'm afraid I'm not going to be able to keep writing you every night like this for the next twelve months. Most nights, after we've finished dinner, the boys have started on their homework, the laundry's been folded and the dogs let out one last time, I'm ready to crawl into bed and watch the latest episode of Snapped.

You have every right to make fun of me for watching that stuff. How is it I'm able to fall asleep, alone in our darkened bedroom, with photos of crime scenes and murder weapons flashing across the TV screen?

I suppose it keeps me from feeling too sorry for myself—whatever kind of day I might've had, the person in the crime scene photos definitely had a shittier day than I did.

Did you remember the boys have the Turnabout dance this weekend? Finn continues to insist he and Crystal are "just friends." Rory, on the other hand, has had a crush on Ashley ever since we moved here. I'll make sure to take lots of photos. The houses where they're meeting before the dance are on opposite sides of town, naturally. If you were here we could tag-team it. But don't worry. I've got this.

I'm anxious to hear back from you about Fakhir—are you having trouble sending emails or something?

Friday, January 18, 2008   12:31 p.m.

Writing this on my lunch break so I'll have to be quick. I can't think of a better way to start the day than waking up to find an email from you. (By the way, is it weird that I've started sleeping with my laptop in addition to my phone?)

I'm happy everything's all right. I know you only had a few minutes, what with a long line of people behind you waiting to use the computer at the USO. I'll take a few brief sentences over radio silence any day.

Maj. Miller called last night just as I was about to fall asleep. He said he was calling to check in on the boys and me, which was awfully nice of him. I got the sense he was feeling a bit lonesome himself (and might've had a few beers under his belt) since he was calling so late. Isabel took the baby to visit her family in New Orleans for a few days, so I invited Wade to Sunday dinner at our house. It'll be good to catch up, hear what's been going on with them since he got out.

I'll be up and ready with my coffee when you call Sunday morning at nine. I like the idea of pre-scheduled phone dates. That way, I don't have to worry about missing a call from you.

And I'm glad you don't think I'm crazy for suggesting Fakhir come live with us. I mentioned the idea to the boys during dinner the other night. Finn seemed fine with it, which is no surprise seeing he's got college coming up in the fall and one foot out the door already. Rory's response was more measured. He wondered if Fakhir staying in the basement would put a crimp on him and his friends hanging out in the TV room. They do spend a lot of time down there playing video games and whatnot. I told him we'd definitely take that into consideration if it's something he's concerned about.

Rory also asked if Fakhir is allergic to animals. I said I had no idea. Then he asks, does he even know we have two dogs, three cats, a lizard and a goldfish? No, I said. I told Rory we're getting ahead of ourselves, we still need to talk things over with Dad. But if we do end up inviting Fakhir to come live with us, Rory's right — we need to be up front with him about the pets. Because, even if Fakhir's not allergic to animals, what if he doesn't like them?

9:56 p.m.

It's our first weekend at home without you. Rory's at the high school playing in a dodgeball tournament and Finn went to a concert downtown. I had a date with Robert Osborne and a bowl of popcorn, watching "Make Way for Tomorrow" on TCM. Have you seen that one? So sad, and probably not the best old movie for me to watch my first Friday night alone. It's about an elderly couple named Barkley and Lucy Cooper (played by Victor Moore and Beulah Bondi) who have to move in with their grown children after the bank forecloses on their house. The husband and wife end up living separately because none of the kids has enough room for both of them. The ending where they say goodbye to each other at the train station makes me cry every time I see it:

Barkley: *In case … I don't see you again …*

Lucy: *What?*

Barkley: *Well, anything might happen. The train could jump off the tracks. If it should happen that I don't see you again, it's been very nice knowing you, Miss Breckenridge.*

Lucy: Bark, that's probably the prettiest speech you ever made. And in case I don't see you ag — well, for a little while. I just want to tell you, it's been lovely, every bit of it, the whole fifty years. I'd sooner have been your wife, Bark, than anyone else on Earth.

I read somewhere the studio pressured the director to make the ending more upbeat, but (luckily for us) the director refused. The ending is perfect just the way it is. Why is it that film studios and book publishers think people only want happy endings? Do they think we're going to fall apart or something if we don't leave the theater or close the book with big happy smiles on our faces? Don't they understand that sometimes, reading a story or watching a movie that makes us weep is a way for us to feel we're not alone?

Saturday, January 19, 2008   7:55 p.m.

I got some good photos of Finn and Rory and their dates before the dance tonight. The day turned out to be a bit more stressful than I anticipated however. For starters, Finn forgot to order flowers for Crystal. Fortunately, when we went to pick up Rory's flowers for Ashley, the florist was kind enough to whip up an extra wrist corsage on the spot. One crisis averted.

I'd had both boys' suits dry cleaned, but forgot to check their ties ahead of time. Finn's tie was already knotted from when he wore it to the Christmas Dance — just loosened and ready to slip over his head. Rory's tie is new, and unfortunately we realized too late that you're the only one around here who knows how to tie a tie. I sure as hell don't know how. (Note to self: Make sure sons know how to tie their own damn ties before Dad leaves on his next deployment.)

Ever the problem-solver, Rory had the brilliant idea to search YouTube for a video on how to tie a necktie. (Thank you Al Gore for inventing the Internet.) It was a little tricky but we ended up bringing my laptop into the bathroom so Rory could watch the video while looking in the mirror and attempting to figure out the loops and twists. When he finally got it right, it was a few minutes past the time he was supposed to leave, and I have to admit we were both getting a little testy. I felt guilty for not knowing how to tie a tie (my lack of such knowledge yet another reason I'll never pass Military Wife 101), and Rory was irritated with me (naturally) for not knowing. And I guess maybe both of us were the tiniest bit mad at you for not being here to help.

By the way, I'm sure these are exactly the types of things I'm not supposed to share with you while you're away, according to the nifty little "deployment guidebook" the military gives us spouses. For example, under "Communicating During Deployment": "*Don't get caught up in negative thinking or emotions. Be honest but tactful. Be careful with sarcasm and humor.*"

Be careful with sarcasm and humor? What fun is that?

Aside from the tie episode, in the rush to help the boys get ready there wasn't much time to dwell on you not being here. Except for when I got to the house where Rory's group had gathered for photos. My throat tightened when I walked in and saw all the other parents laughing and socializing amongst themselves, as if they didn't have a care in the world. Do they not know there's a war going on? As I stood alone watching Rory and his friends all dressed up and excited for the dance, my eyes filled with tears thinking of you, a thousand miles away (and soon to be six thousand miles away).

I know we had our reasons for choosing to live off base this time around, but this was one instance I longed to be surrounded by other military families instead of bankers and lawyers and orthodontists. Certainly most of them knew that less than a week ago the boys and I said goodbye to you. Standing there alone, without you, I wondered: Why is no one asking me about you? Or asking how the boys are doing? In fact, why is no one talking to me at all? Is it that they don't know what to say? Or perhaps I'm an uncomfortable reminder of something they'd rather not think about on a Saturday night?

I admit to feeling more than a little sorry for myself as I stood off to the side of the group, smiling awkwardly in case anyone happened to catch my eye (no one did). But mostly my thoughts were of you, knowing how much you would've enjoyed being there, taking photos of Rory and his date. I felt bad you had to miss it, and sorry for the boys that they couldn't have their dad be a part of this moment.

Thankfully Rory was too busy making goo-goo eyes at Ashley to notice me getting all sentimental. Also, I'm sure any sadness he might've felt about you not being there dissipated the moment he laid eyes on his date. (You'll understand when you look at the photos.)

I snapped a few pictures of Rory and Ashley, gave Rory a hug and reminded him to check in with me once they arrived at the dance. I made my way toward the door and was just about to make my getaway to Finn's photo session when I realized I was being followed by Agnes Hawkins, who proceeded to corner me in the foyer. Here I'd just spent the last fifteen minutes wishing somebody would talk to me, but really? Of all people, why did it have to be Agnes?

"There you are!" she calls after me, just as I have my hand on the doorknob. "I'm not going to let you get away without saying hello."

Oh shit, I think to myself. This is the last person I need to be talking to right now. "Hello Agnes," I say, managing a smile while at the same time keeping my hand on the doorknob. "I was just on my way to Finn's photo session," I explain, nodding my head in the direction I want to be going right now, which is pretty much anywhere but here.

"I'll only keep you a minute," she says.

Yeah right. I suddenly feel underdressed as I tighten my winter coat over my sweatshirt and jeans, noticing she's wearing a dress and high heels even though there's a foot of snow outside and we're not the ones going to the dance.

As if reading my mind, her eyes come to rest on my jeans, which are bunched up above my snow boots. She tears her gaze away from my attire long enough to look me in the eye. "Now Emilie. I'm hosting a fundraiser for Congressman Roper in a few weeks and I thought you'd be just the person to help me organize it. You know, make calls to donors and whip up some finger foods and things like that."

"Oh, I'm sorry Agnes, but I won't have much free time now that Liam's not here. What with work, and keeping an eye on the boys, and taking care of the house ..."

"Oh come now," she says. "You can't tell me you don't have all *kinds* of free time on your hands now that Liam's gone? I'd give *anything* to have that pesky husband of mine out of my hair for a few months — aren't you the luckiest thing ever!" At this she cackles loudly, and I find myself wondering if this is what it sounds like when a chicken is in respiratory distress.

I massage the back of my neck in an effort to keep my hand from reaching out and yanking on that fake-looking red hair of hers. Anything to stop her from making that awful clucking sound. Does she really think this is going to be some sort of fun vacation for you and me, where I'm just sitting around at home twiddling my thumbs looking for shit to do?

Much as I'd like to tell Agnes to go fuck herself, I instead manage to say, "Well, good luck with the fundraiser Agnes. I've gotta run." I quickly swing open the door and step outside before Agnes can say anything further (although I'm pretty sure I can hear her talking as I slam the door shut behind me).

Thankfully, in the few minutes it takes me to drive to Crystal's house, I'm able to get a hold of myself. I step inside the foyer and immediately feel more at ease. The mood here is downright boisterous. Three years older than the freshman I'd just left, this group of seniors has been to a dozen dances by now — not the least bit nervous or self-conscious. They mingle easily with the parents and amongst themselves. I take a calming breath and soak in every detail, knowing this will be Finn's last Turnabout Dance. Finn spots me from across the room and quickly makes his way toward me. He gives me a kiss and a hug and pulls me over to chat with him and Crystal and Neil and Darryl and their dates.

I'm sending along a few of the photos I took. Both boys looked dashingly handsome of course — just like their dad.

I can't wait to talk to you in the morning. I'm sure by then I'll have thought of all the brilliant comebacks I wish I'd said to Agnes.

Sunday, January 20, 2008   9:33 a.m.

Just hung up the phone with you. The boys are still asleep, I'm on my second cup of coffee, and Soda and Brig have finally decided to relax after having been let out three times to bark at the squirrels.

Now that we've spoken, I can see why you'd want us to do our part by helping Fakhir. I had no idea how much assistance he's given our Marines in Iraq the last several years. Or the extent to which he's risked his life and his family's safety by serving as an interpreter. I also didn't realize you knew him as well as you do. Talking to you about it has made me even more excited to support him in his transition here. I'll run it by the boys again this afternoon and, if they agree it's a good thing for all of us, I'll call Fakhir at the Salazars' after dinner tonight.

I'm glad things are going well for you in California, but it sounds like there's still a lot to accomplish before you leave. All the medical tests, immunizations, safety briefs, checking and rechecking of weapons. The way you described the process of gathering the necessary supplies for your deployment was interesting to me. Going through a warehouse with a giant shopping cart and a checklist? Kinda reminds me of one of our trips to Costco — minus the guns and gas masks. I don't suppose you get free samples of Taquitos and spinach-stuffed raviolis while you're strolling through the weapons arsenal?

No wonder you're anxious to be done with all the pre-deployment stuff and just get over there. The waiting must be nerve-wracking for you. If it weren't for the boys, I wish I could go with you. I know that sounds insane. But here you are, going out into the world to do something meaningful and important, while I stay back here folding laundry and scooping cat poop out of litter boxes. Is there room on the C-5 for someone with a degree in Comparative Literature, who can also type 90 words a minute? In my heart I know you'd much rather stay here at home with us. And I realize the coming year will be anything but pleasant for you. But I have to wonder, is there a tiny piece inside you hungry for the experiences that await?

11:19 p.m.

Fakhir seemed genuinely touched when I called tonight to invite him to stay with us. We talked about him moving here pretty quickly since the Salazars are PCSing soon and things are already in flux at their house. He doesn't have many belongings with him so he may start living here as early as next week — after we return from Rory's hockey tournament in Chicago. The only thing is, I was so charged up during our conversation I forgot to mention about the pets. I'll be sure to bring it up next time we talk.

I did remember to ask Rory if he still has concerns about Fakhir staying in the basement, right next to the TV room. To my surprise, Rory said he thought it over, and he's perfectly fine now with Fakhir using that room down there. (Between you and me, I think what really happened is that Rory told his friends a Marine interpreter might be living in our basement, and, as might be expected of 14-year-old boys, they got all keyed up talking about how badass that's going to be.)

As a matter of fact, both boys suddenly seem pumped about this whole thing. I'm not sure why, though it might have something to do with "restoring the testosterone level around this place" — which, according to them, has been out of whack since you left. (At any rate, I'm outnumbered here no matter how you slice it.)

Speaking of testosterone, there was plenty of it around the dinner table tonight with Wade Miller as our guest. It was too cold out to grill so we cooked steaks in the broiler. We also had baked potatoes and a salad. Wade brought a bottle of red wine, most of which he drank himself.

He regaled the boys with stories of his deployments to Iraq and Afghanistan, which they found fascinating and highly amusing. (Like the time he went to the bazaar in Mosul and got bit in the ass by a camel. Remember that story? It gets funnier every time he tells it.) Wade even talked a bit about his first time in Fallujah in '04, which I'd never heard him speak of until now. Listening to Wade's stories made it feel as if a part of you was with us tonight.

He had a lot of good things to say about Fakhir too. According to Wade, Fakhir worked as his interpreter on a number of combat missions during Wade's three tours there. The more I hear about Fakhir, the more it seems he gets around.

Wade furthermore couldn't pass up the opportunity to give me shit about the little mix-up we had before you left. You know, the one where I asked you to stop at the PX on your way home from work and pick up one of those gold star flags so I could hang it in the window while you're gone? Obviously, I know the difference between a gold star and a blue star. I mean, Hell's bells! You've been deployed — what — a dozen times now? And, every single one of those deployments we've had the blue star flag in our window. It's not my fault I couldn't find the damn thing in any of our moving boxes. I have no fucking idea what I was thinking that morning when I asked you to get me the gold star flag. At least I didn't mind that you found the whole thing absolutely hilarious. Except that, as soon as you got to work that day, you told everyone in the unit about it — including Gen. Lewis.

As Wade tells the story to Rory and Finn (even though they already know the whole thing verbatim), I rest my elbows on the table and make a steeple with my fingers, waiting patiently for him to finish. "And how is it that you heard about this Wade, since it happened in December and you retired the month before?" I ask.

"Word gets around," he says, taking a sip of wine and smiling enigmatically.

I turn to the boys in an attempt to explain myself. "I honestly can't tell you guys what I was thinking that morning. I do know that all of us were stretched to our limit the month before Dad left. He and I were making all those trips to the lawyer's office to update Dad's will and power of attorney and medical directive and all that. And then we had those insurance people coming to the house to do medical check-ups or whatever so Dad could buy more life insurance. Between that and everything else going on ... last month was brutal. I guess my brain was totally fried."

"I'll say," Finn replies. "Like when you wore two different shoes to work the week before he left?"

I glance at Wade, embarrassed, yet concede this little tidbit with a shrug.

"Yeah," Rory chimes in. "And when you forgot where you hid half our Christmas presents? Have you found those yet by the way?"

"No," I sheepishly admit. "I'm sorry. I still can't remember where I put them. Dad's been on tons of deployments, but that doesn't mean it gets any easier, right?"

The boys nod in agreement.

"You two have been great though," I say to Finn and Rory. "Thank you for that. As for me, well … let's just say I'm never going to be nominated for Military Spouse of the Year."

"Mom, you keep saying that, but it's not true," Rory says. "You're the best."

I smile but say nothing, due to the lump in my throat.

Wade finishes off the wine in his glass and sets it down. "Ahh, you don't need that Military Spouse of the Year shit," he says, grabbing my hand. "You're a stealth wife. You may not show up at all the FSG meetings or get involved in what's going on at the unit. But Liam knows how much you do to hold things together at home. He talks about you, a lot. And yeah, he likes to poke fun at you sometimes. But he also makes sure to let everyone know how strong you are, and that he couldn't do his job without you."

"That's just the wine talking," I say, tilting my head toward the empty bottle. My eyes are getting teary and I feel a full-blown cry session coming on so I abruptly get up from the table and signal the boys to start helping me clear the plates.

"Here, let me help with those," Wade says. He stands up a little too quickly, grabbing the table to steady himself. "Whoa. Head rush."

"No, no — we'll take care of this," I say to Wade, putting my hand on his shoulder. "In fact, how about if I drive you home in your car. Finn can follow behind us in our car and give me a lift back."

"Totally not necessary," Wade replies, still leaning unsteadily on the table.

I put my hand out, palm up, holding Wade's gaze.

"Geez! I can see there's no arguing with you." He fishes in the front pocket of his jeans for his car keys and places them in my out-stretched hand.

I smile at Wade, then ask Rory to finish up the dishes while Finn and I make the short trip to Wade's house and back. It's a good thing Isabel is out of town with Chloe. I don't think she'd be too happy with Wade coming home intoxicated. Again.

I'm glad Wade handed over his car keys though. The last thing he needs right now is another DUI. Still, it was nice having him here. Except it made me miss you even more.

Monday, January 21, 2008   11:04 p.m.

I forgot there was no school today. My alarm went off at 0530 as usual. I got up, let the dogs out, fed all the pets, made my coffee, got the paper, and took my shower. When I was putting on my makeup I realized the boys weren't getting out of bed at their usual time. So I went in Rory's room and asked why he and his brother were still sleeping. To say he was pissed at me for waking him up would be an understatement. Yet I would like to point out he had no trouble falling back asleep after reminding me it was Martin Luther King Day.

I used the unexpected free time to start cleaning up the guest room for Fakhir. The bed and dresser down there will suffice. I don't know if you recall, but we've been using that room as a catch-all for miscella-neous crap. Like your giant box of extension cords. (Explain to me again why we need so many extension cords?) And the rolled-up rugs from our last house on base that don't fit the rooms in this house. I promise not to get rid of your precious extension cord collection but I *am* giving the rugs to Goodwill.

I called Fakhir back tonight to nail down some details and talk about the pets. He's moving in a week from Wednesday. That will give me next Monday and Tuesday nights to make sure all our ducks are in a row before he gets here. Rory and I won't get home from the hockey tournament until late Sunday, so next weekend is shot as far as getting any cleaning done.

Before I called Fakhir I called the Salazar's house phone to talk to Janet about the pets. She says Fakhir has gotten used to their German Shepherd, but she admits he might be a bit overwhelmed at first with the sheer number of pets at our house. (I mean, who wouldn't?) But she assured me she didn't think the pets would pose any major problems for Fakhir. God I hope not.

After Fakhir and I figured out the details for next week, I switched gears and asked him if he had any pets as a kid. He told me he and his sisters did have a dog growing up — in fact the dog still lives with his mom and sisters at their house in Baghdad. But it's an outside dog.

"Well, the situation at our house is a little different than that," I explain. "We've got two dogs — a Chihuahua named Soda and a terrier named Brig. They're inside dogs. And then there's the three cats — Smedley, Button, and Daly. They're inside pets too. Oh, and in Rory's room there's a bearded dragon named Ozzy and a goldfish named Elvis."

Fakhir whistles softly into the phone. "That's a lot of pets," he says. Then, "And you have a dragon too?"

"Well, it's actually a lizard. They're called bearded dragons. But they're lizards. If that makes any sense."

"I see," he replies. He sounds hesitant. I can almost hear the gears turning inside his head as he works through this information.

"Would you like to come over to meet the pets before you move in next week?" I ask.

"That's very kind of you to offer ma'am, but it won't be necessary," he says.

"Fakhir, if you're going to live at our house, no way in hell can you keep calling me 'ma'am.'"

He laughs. "Got it, Mrs. Mahoney."

"Nice try. But that's not going to fly either. It's Emilie, okay?"

"Message heard and received ... Emilie," he replies. Then, taking a deep breath, he says, "I'm sure I'll be fine with the pets."

"We can always take things slow."

"Right." His tone suddenly turns cheerful. "Some people say you can't change an old dog's spots but I'm not old and I can definitely change my spots." He chuckles at his own cleverness.

Liam, do you think I should have told Fakhir he was mixing up his metaphors? I didn't want to be impolite by correcting him. But he probably meant, "you can't teach an old dog new tricks," right? Or do you think he meant, "a leopard can't change its spots?"

No matter. I knew what he was trying to say. And given time, I'm sure he'll grow to love the pets.

But what if they don't love him back?

Tuesday, January 22, 2008   10:46 p.m.

I'm hosting book club tomorrow night so I'll have to make this short — just finished cleaning the family room and whipping up a few appetizers. (BTW, I miss having you here as my sous chef to clean up all the messes I make when I cook.) Fridge is stocked with wine and beer and I'm getting ready to print off my author research. We're discussing Leif Enger's *Peace Like A River*. (I loved it. Do you want me to send it to you?)

Finn had his piano lesson after school. I admit to staying within earshot (as in, busying myself in the kitchen) when Mr. Lavin is here. That way I can listen to his soft Irish brogue and Finn's piano playing, both of which give me tingles. Finn is working on Chopin's Nocturne in E Flat Major and it's coming along well. The recital isn't 'til the end of March, which gives him plenty of time to memorize it.

Speaking of music, have you had a chance to use the iPod nano we bought you for Christmas? (Luckily that wasn't one of the gifts I misplaced.) The boys and I thought listening to music while you run would help make the time go by faster. I hope you'll be able to find a safe running route once you land in Iraq.

Rory had an extra long hockey practice tonight to get ready for this weekend's tournament in Chicago. It's been a while since I've traveled alone with him to a tournament. I hope I can be half as good a hockey dad as you are.

The clock is ticking and I guess you'll be leaving for Iraq sometime next week. I know you can't say anything in email, so I hope you're able to call on a secure line before you leave. It would be nice to have at least a general idea of your departure plans. It's a good thing Rory and I will be traveling to Chicago this weekend. Being busy might help me not worry so much about you. Once your plane leaves U.S. soil, this all becomes a little too real.

Wednesday, January 23, 2008   11:41 p.m.

Book club went well tonight. My stuffed mushrooms, rumaki, and artichoke dip were a hit. (Between you and me, the dip came from Costco. I just jazzed it up with some chopped green chiles and extra Parmesan.) Our discussion was great, as always. (It's pretty unusual to be part of a book club that actually talks about the book — especially since there's alcohol involved.) Though I have to tell you, Agnes Hawkins was up to her usual shenanigans, trying to pretend she'd read the book when it was obvious she hadn't. Except tonight, Barb called her out on it. Agnes doubled down and insisted she *had* read the book. Watching her try to wriggle her way out of that one was the highlight of the evening.

It's been a long day. Rory woke me before my alarm went off to tell me he forgot to bring home his Biology book and could I please take him to school early so he can finish today's assignment before first period. He usually doesn't like being seen riding to school with me (and who can blame him — I *am* the ISS Supervisor after all), but desperate times call for desperate measures.

I had only one student in ISS today but boy was she a handful. Most of the time it's the boys who get In-School Suspension. But when I do get girls, they tend to be humdingers — and today was no exception. When she arrived this morning, her mascara was already streaked from crying. And to make certain I knew she was unhappy about being there, she made a show of throwing her backpack into the study carrel — a childish gesture which I chose to ignore. I introduced myself and extended my hand for her to shake, which she in turn ignored. So I ignored her ignoring me, and went over the ISS rules with her instead.

I told her I was there to help her have a productive time and that I hoped she'd feel better by the end of the day, ready to go back to class tomorrow with a new perspective. I was trying my best to be cordial but she wasn't making it easy. Her write-up said she'd been disrespecting a teacher, talking back and disrupting the class, so the administrator thought it best to put her in my room for a day. Yay me. I printed out the list of assignments from her teachers and explained today would be a good opportunity for her to get caught up on schoolwork.

No sooner had I gone back to my desk than I notice she has one hand inside her purse (which was hanging off the back of her chair) and she's staring down into it as if hypnotized by some magical force. Texting, obviously — with cell phone usage being one of the forbidden things in the rules we'd just gone over.

"Lucia, please remove your phone from your purse, turn it off, and set it on the shelf above your study carrel where I can see it."

Big dramatic sigh. "I wasn't even looking at my phone," she argues.

"Regardless, the phone needs to be off and in my line of sight."

Another big sigh, but at least she removes her phone from her purse, turns it off, and tosses it (angrily) on the shelf. She then turns her back to me, grabs a book out of her backpack, opens the book, hunches over it, and appears to be reading.

The problem now is that I'm having to contend with her low-riding jeans, which reveal a full-on view of her animal-print thong as well as a good portion of her butt crack. (I have this issue with the boys too but boxer shorts, generally speaking, don't show as much crack. Either way — not something I want to be staring at all day.)

"Lucia, are you aware that your underwear is showing?"

She turns around in her chair to look at me. "Is that a problem?"

"Why yes, as a matter of fact it is. I see you've brought a hoodie with you. How about if you put that on?"

"I'm not cold."

"I guess you'd prefer to be sent home to change then, which would probably earn you another day here with me in ISS?" I smile pleasantly.

Another long, dramatic sigh. She turns back around and grudgingly puts on the hoodie (which adequately covers her rear), and resumes reading. Butt-crack problem solved.

I return to my work. A few minutes later I hear a crinkling sound. I look up to see Lucia surreptitiously grabbing Skittles out of her hoodie pocket, and slowly putting them in her mouth as she continues reading, being careful to chew as quietly as possible.

I watch her for a moment, then raise my eyes to the ceiling and count to ten. Although eating candy is against the rules, she is reading her book. Quietly. I decide to let her be — for now.

When I take her to the cafeteria at lunchtime, she refuses to eat. I ask her if she brought a sack lunch and she says no. I ask her if she wants to buy something at the lunch counter and she says she's not hungry. (Who knew Skittles could be so filling?)

So we go back to the ISS room where I offer her half of my peanut butter & jelly sandwich plus half my bag of potato chips and half an orange. She refuses but I place the food on a napkin and leave it in her study carrel anyway. I return to my own desk, where I continue with what I was working on before lunch, holding my half of the sandwich in one hand while making notes on a legal pad with the other.

The next time I glance up, I can see she's finished the chips and is starting on the sandwich. I pretend not to notice and resume my work.

Next time I look up, the sandwich is gone and she's methodically eating one orange segment at a time.

My guess? She doesn't have any money in her lunch account and there's not enough food in the fridge at home for her to take a lunch to school. I return to my work without saying anything.

A while later, without turning around, she says, "I like your eye make-up." (I happened to be wearing my electric blue eyeliner with sparkly charcoal eye shadow today.)

"Thanks." I look up from what I'm doing and turn my chair toward her. "It's NYX. I got it from the Ulta store downtown."

She quickly turns around in her chair, her interest piqued. "I bet it was expensive though."

"No, not really. The eye shadow was like $3.99 and the liner was $2.99."

"For real? That looks like some expensive shit — uh, stuff."

We get to talking about make-up and I come to find out she wants to go to cosmetology school after graduation. We have a nice little chat about that and before I know it she ends up apologizing to me. "I'm sorry I was being mean to you this morning," she says. "This is my first time in ISS and I thought you were going to be mean to me. So I decided to be mean to you first. But you're not mean at all."

"Thanks Lucia. That's nice of you to say. And I accept your apology. Now which of those assignments do you still need to finish?"

Liam, you know this job isn't exactly what I dreamed I'd be doing at this point in my life. It's not even remotely related to my degree. But on days like today I'm happy I took the job. I like working with the students, helping them get back on track. And it's good having some structure to my day, especially now that you're gone. I don't make much, but the money I do make will help when Finn goes off to college. It's been hard for me to build a career what with us moving every few years. A lot of places won't even hire military spouses, knowing we won't be around for long. At least here, they gave me a chance.

Thursday, January 24, 2008   9:18 p.m.

Just finished a bunch of laundry, including Rory's hockey pants, jerseys, and socks, plus I threw in his knee, shoulder, and elbow pads for good measure. That familiar yet uniquely sour smell emanating from his hockey bag was getting a little too pungent, even for the garage. No wonder the hotels won't let our kids keep equipment in the rooms.

Rory and I leave early tomorrow morning, which will put us in Chicago with just enough time to head straight to the rink tomorrow night. I'll email you sometime over the weekend to let you know how the games are going. They have one game Friday night, two Saturday, and one Sunday morning. I hear there's talk of a snowstorm in the Midwest Sunday afternoon; I hope we'll be able to get ahead of any inclement weather.

I'm looking forward to spending some quality time with Rory. Finn said he didn't want to take off work this weekend, so he's staying back here. Besides, we needed someone to take care of the pets. I told him he could have a few friends in the house while we're gone but no more than three or four. And absolutely no alcohol. I also told him I expect to come back to a house that's as clean as I left it. I don't want Fakhir thinking we're barbarians when he walks in the door Wednesday night.

I wish you were coming with us to the tournament.

Saturday, January 26, 2008   10:22 a.m.

Boy do I feel like a heel. Don't worry — we arrived in Chicago safe and sound yesterday. (And I'm sorry I didn't write last night to tell you so.) They did win their game, and Rory played well — he got two assists and no penalties. So everything is fine in that department. It's just that it turns out I'm not a very good replacement when it comes to you and the routine you and Rory have on these hockey trips.

The car ride yesterday was enjoyable — we had a nice time talking and listening to music. I had a couple beers in the hotel lobby with the other parents after the game last night while Rory and his teammates swam in the pool. Everything seemed fine.

But this morning when everybody met in the lobby for breakfast, Rory was just plain grumpy.

First thing he does is tell me my snow boots look "dorky" and that I should go put on some "normal" shoes. "I thought you liked these boots?" I say. He rolls his eyes and turns his back to me.

In the buffet line when I grab fruit and yogurt he tells me I should have oatmeal because "that's what Dad usually has." So I put my yogurt back and say, "How about if we both have oatmeal — in honor of Dad?" That manages to put a small smile on his face, much as he tries to resist.

I know he's just missing you so I'm trying not to take his grumpiness too personally. But then when I went to hug him and wish him luck before the game outside the rink just a while ago, he steps back and waves me off as if I had just vomited on my shirt or something. Thing is, I always give him a pre-game hug. I know he's not trying to be mean — but that hurt. He's probably feeling a little uncertain, this being the first in a long line of tournaments he'll play this year without you here to cheer him on. It's got to be hard on him.

Maybe it was me who needed the hug more than him.

The players are in the locker room now and the game begins in less than 20 minutes. I'm typing this from my laptop in the car, where I can still get the Wi-Fi signal from the rink. I just needed a few minutes alone to gather my thoughts and pull myself together. If Rory and Finn can be grumpy to me when they're missing you, who do I get to be grumpy to?

Monday, January 28, 2008   9:38 p.m.

I'm sorry I didn't write last night. We ended up smack dab in the middle of that snowstorm coming home from Chicago yesterday. We're fine, but Rory and I didn't get home until 3 a.m. and we still had to get up for school and work this morning, (No school cancellations here, unfortunately). The roads were a sheet of ice between Chicago and Des Moines. I thought about pulling off the highway and just staying at a hotel for the night but every off-ramp we passed was filled with jack-knifed semis and cars that had skidded off the road. So we figured it was safer to just keep inching forward with all the other cars.

I could see Rory getting sleepy but he forced himself to stay awake to keep me company. We entertained ourselves by singing every patriotic song we could think of: Star Spangled Banner, My Country 'Tis of Thee, Yankee Doodle Dandy, You're A Grand Old Flag, and This Land is Your Land. You should have heard us. Rory didn't even make fun of my terrible singing voice (which I know you guys do behind my back).

Eventually around midnight we passed through Des Moines and made it out of the worst of the storm. The roads were mostly clear the rest of the way home. After we stopped singing, Rory told me Ashley had broken up with him this weekend via text. (That was a brief romance.) She told him she's now going out with a guy on the basketball team. I told Rory I was sorry. I know he liked her a lot. But he's young and there will be other girls. Lots of other girls. He can't see that now though. Poor guy.

We were still a couple hours from home when Rory couldn't keep his eyes open any longer. I told him to get some rest. No use both of us being exhausted. (Besides, I needed some quiet time to plot my revenge against Ashley for breaking Rory's heart. Just kidding. Sort of.)

We went straight to bed as soon as we got home and I was so tired this morning I didn't notice the condition of the house before I left for work. While he must have attempted to do *some* cleanup, it appears Finn had more than a few friends over this weekend.

My first clue when I got home from work today was the discovery of female clothing in our laundry basket — clothing belonging to Someone Other Than Your Wife Who Is Not A Size 2. That set off my radar and I began to notice all the other things I was too tired to catch last night and this morning. Like the sticky hardwood floor in the foyer and the pictures askew in the hallway. And the unmistakable smell of alcohol in the blender when I went to make myself a smoothie. The clincher came when I plopped down on the family room couch to collect my thoughts. I'm sitting there, drinking my smoothie, when I feel something lumpy against my back. I reach behind me to fluff up the pillow and lo and behold what do I find but an empty bottle of Captain Morgan spiced rum.

As you can imagine we had quite the shitstorm here after Finn got home from work tonight. During which, I might add, I raised my voice and probably said a few things I shouldn't have.

"Rory, would you mind finishing your homework upstairs tonight?" I ask. "I have something I need to chat with Finn about. In private."

Rory grumbles something about always being left out of the good stuff but collects his books and papers and exits the kitchen. Finn, who's sitting at the table across from me, appears to have become suddenly paralyzed, the hand holding a cookie he was about to take a bite of frozen halfway between the table and his mouth.

I wait, listening as Rory drags himself up the stairs. Once I'm certain he's out of earshot, I look Finn in the eye. "So. I guess you had a party here while Rory and I were in Chicago."

Finn carefully sets down the cookie and arranges his face into a look of complete innocence. "What? I didn't have a party here."

I hold Finn's gaze and he holds mine right back without blinking. This kid could have a stellar career with the CIA. I wait a few more seconds, and when he still doesn't look away I say, "I'm giving you a chance to be truthful here, Finn."

"Mom, I swear, I did *not* have a party."

"Then explain to me why I found some random girl's sweater in our laundry basket?"

"Oh," Finn says, leaning back in his chair and opening his palms as if to say, well that explains everything. "That's Crystal's. She asked me to wash it for her."

"Finn, you don't even do your own laundry. You expect me to believe you agreed to do Crystal's laundry? And, why would she be taking off her sweater at our house anyway? Wait. Don't answer that."

"All right, yes. Crystal did accidentally leave her sweater here," he reasons. "But I don't know why you think that means I had a party."

"Um, how about all the pictures in the front hallway that are tilted this way and that?"

"Pssh," Finn waves his hand dismissively. "That must have happened when I was doing some dusting for you on Saturday. I know how you like the tops of the picture frames dusted."

This almost makes me laugh — if it weren't for the fact I'm becoming increasingly pissed off. "So. You dusted the picture frames but you somehow missed the floor, which is totally sticky?"

He opens his mouth to speak but I raise my hand. "Just shut your pie-hole Finn. I've had enough of your MUSADI."

"Mom, I am *not* MUSADI-ing!" he protests.

"Then how do you explain the fact that my blender smells like some-one's been making pina coladas in it all weekend?"

"Pineapple smoothies?" he offers weakly.

"Right. And the empty bottle of Captain Morgan I found stuffed behind a pillow on the family room couch?"

"Shit," he whispers under his breath. Caught red-handed, he smartly concedes the evidence doesn't lie and therefore tries a different tack. "You did tell me I could have a few friends over."

"I specifically said you could have three or four friends over. Not three or four *hundred*." My voice is getting louder.

"Mom, no way were there four hundred people here this weekend. Maybe like, fifty. Or a hundred. But not four hundred."

"Oh. That's just great!" I'm yelling now but I can't help myself. "I cannot believe you had a hundred people here! You're lucky the cops didn't come!"

"Maybe it was more like seventy-five," he assures me. As if that's going to make me feel better. "But we were very careful," he continues. "Everybody parked their cars on the other side of the block and came through the back yard. Nobody even used the front door."

"How considerate of you. The thing is, you are all underage! And you were drinking! In *our* house! While Dad's about to leave for Iraq!" I'm practically screaming now.

Finn has finally come to the realization he's in big-ass trouble. Wisely, he keeps his trap shut as I struggle to regain my composure.

I exhale loudly through my nose, trying to shake off my anger. In a quiet voice I say, "You have disrespected our house rules and broken my trust. Dad hasn't even left for Iraq yet. This behavior is totally unsat, and I am not going to put up with it while Dad's gone. There's going to be some changes around here and for starters you are grounded for at *least* the next two weeks. Now how about you un-ass yourself and go to your room before I lose my temper. Again."

Finn quickly gets his butt out of the chair and retreats to his room. I sit at the kitchen table, hands clenched, trying to pull myself off the ceiling.

Now I'm wondering if I should even send this email to you. Maybe I should just delete it. But we did make the agreement before you left to be as honest as possible with each other—without violating OPSEC of course. And yet … I don't know if I should be dumping on you like this at such a critical time, when you could be going in-country any day now. (Shit, did I just violate OPSEC?) I can't even think straight anymore. Fuck it. I'm sending this.

Tuesday, January 29, 2008   11:41 p.m.

Thank you for calling last night. I'm sorry for worrying you. It was selfish of me to unload on you like that. I apologize.

And thank you for talking to Finn and Rory and reminding them to step up to the plate while you're gone. Hearing your calm and reassuring voice was a wake-up call for all three of us. I realize the boys don't mean to be irresponsible or thoughtless. They are teenagers after all. They don't say as much, but I know this deployment isn't easy for them. I'm the adult and I need to be the one who sets the tone around here.

I started a new ritual tonight: I'm taking Finn and Rory out to dinner one night a week, where we can get caught up in a more relaxed environment, without the distractions of home. I'm hoping it will help the boys and me stay connected while you're away. And besides, you and I won't be spending money on date nights the next twelve months, so I figure our budget can handle it.

We went to Lemongrass for fresh basil chicken and fried rice. Before we got in the car, Finn pulled me aside to apologize for having the party—and more importantly—for lying about it. After we got home they both helped me finish cleaning the guest bedroom for Fakhir. And just when I was about to turn off my light and go to sleep, Rory came in to give me a hug and a kiss goodnight.

I'm a shit for complaining to you about not getting one measly hug from Rory this weekend. You've got more than a year ahead of you with no hugs from anyone.

Wednesday, January 30, 2008   11:27 p.m.

Everyone is settled in for the night, including Fakhir. I'm happy to report we survived our first evening together—though I can't say it went exactly as planned.

Janet and Ray dropped off Fakhir and his luggage after dinner. Before he arrived, I put Soda and Brig in the laundry room so they wouldn't cause a ruckus when he got here. That would have worked well except one of the boys accidentally opened the laundry room door within moments of his arrival. The dogs, naturally, made a beeline for Fakhir as he stood helplessly in the foyer. Brig let loose with her piercing terrier bark and—in true Killer Chihuahua fashion—Soda lunged for Fakhir's kneecaps.

We all know Soda is basically harmless, but I'll admit it's not the most relaxing thing in the world to have a Chihuahua hanging off your pant leg. Poor Fakhir. He tried to be good-natured about it but I could see he was a bit unnerved. Rory quickly moved to extricate Soda from Fakhir's khakis, and luckily, Finn was able to get Brig to calm down as well.

The situation in hand, I proceeded to introduce Fakhir to the boys. Keeping one eye on Soda, he greeted each of them warmly with a smile and a handshake. Soda, meanwhile, parked himself on the floor a few feet away, returning Fakhir's sidelong glances with equal suspicion.

We were still standing in the foyer when the doorbell rang. The boys and I exchange curious glances; we weren't expecting anyone besides Fakhir. So I open the front door, and who do we find standing on our front porch, wearing a lime green pantsuit with matching lime green heels (and no coat, in the dead of winter), but Agnes Hawkins. Holding a plate of brownies.

Had I told Agnes that Fakhir was coming tonight? No, I'm quite sure I didn't. Oh—I know. I must have said something about it at book club last week. Yet I'm certain I didn't mention the exact day he was coming. She must have been watching our house from her living room window this entire week, waiting for Fakhir's arrival. (Which makes me wonder: Where was Agnes last weekend when Finn was entertaining 400 of his closest friends at our house while Rory and I were in Chicago?)

"Hello Agnes," I say, holding the door only partway open in the hope that she'll hand me the brownies and leave. "This is … unexpected."

Nimbly shifting the brownies from one hand to the other, Agnes quickly pulls the door open and steps inside. I have no choice but to step aside lest she knock me over. "I wanted to be the first person in the neighborhood to welcome your new Iraqi houseguest," she announces, her head swiveling from side to side, surveying the inside of our house as if sweeping for landmines. Soda, still stationed in his spot near Fakhir, emits a low growl in Agnes' direction.

Right, I think to myself. What you really mean is that you wanted to be the first person in the neighborhood to get an up-close look at our new houseguest.

"How thoughtful of you," I say, holding the plate of brownies Agnes has now handed me. "Agnes, I'd like you to meet Fakhir. He's going to be living with us the next few months. Fakhir, this is our neighbor Agnes. She lives across the street."

Fakhir smiles politely, extends his hand, and says, "Very nice to meet you Agnes."

She takes his hand in both of hers and, smiling widely, says, "So nice to meet you Fucker."

Fakhir maintains a poker face but the boys' mouths make little O's.

As tactfully as possible I attempt to correct her. "Um, Agnes, his name is FAH-keer."

"That's what I said," she replies, still smiling. Then, turning back to Fakhir and speaking more slowly this time, she repeats, "It's. Very. Nice. To meet you. FUH-ker."

Finn now has his arms folded across his chest, one hand raised to his mouth in an attempt to squeeze the smile off his lips. Rory meanwhile has turned his upper body completely toward the kitchen, as if something of great importance has caught his attention.

This time Fakhir takes a stab at demonstrating how his name is pronounced. Smiling helpfully he says, "Don't worry. A lot of Americans mispronounce my name at first. Try it like this: FAAAAH-keer." He drags out the first syllable for emphasis.

Agnes' smile has faded somewhat and she looks a bit puzzled as to what all the fuss is about. "Okay. I think I've got it now. Nice to meet you, Fuuuucker."

Fakhir maintains a pleasant expression but I can only imagine what's going through his mind. "It may take some practice," he offers.

Desperate to put an end to everyone's misery, I blurt, "How about if you guys take a seat in the family room? I'll go into the kitchen and get us some water." I hand the plate of brownies to Rory, motioning them toward the family room, as I retreat to the kitchen.

I immediately regret inviting Agnes to stay, yet I see no other option than to embrace the suck. I feel bad about leaving the boys and Fakhir to deal with her on their own—even if only for a few minutes. Nonetheless, I briefly consider climbing out the kitchen window and making a run for it. Instead, I grab a tray and some glasses from the cabinet.

As I'm filling the water glasses at the kitchen sink, I can hear Agnes from the family room. She's talking to Fakhir in a really loud voice—like the way you would talk to your 90-year-old great-grandmother who's hard of hearing. Evidently she's under the mistaken impression he doesn't understand English very well (even though I did tell everyone at book club he's an interpreter). She's obviously one of those people who thinks if you talk REALLY LOUDLY it will help the other person understand your English better.

So I get myself back into the family room ricky-tick, being careful not to spill the tray of water glasses. With a tight smile I hand Agnes her glass and say, "Agnes, Fakhir's hearing is fine. There's no need to shout."

I glance quickly at Fakhir, who's looking at me as if to ask, "Who the hell is this person?" I can only shrug apologetically and hope he sees the panicked "I'm so sorry!" look in my eyes as I hand him his glass of water. The boys take their drinks from the tray, and I take a seat across from Agnes and Fakhir, who are sitting side-by-side on the couch.

Agnes takes a sip of her water and, looking at Fakhir, she points to her water glass and enunciates very slowly, "wwwaaaater." "This is called wwwaaaater."

What the fuck? Does she think Fakhir is Helen Keller or something? By this time Finn and Rory are about to bust a gut and I can hardly even look at the two of them for fear I'll start laughing too. Fakhir's eyes have gotten even wider and he's again looking at me, no doubt wondering what the hell should he say to this crazy-pants sitting in our family room.

I clear my throat. "Agnes. Fakhir speaks Arabic, English, *and* Spanish. Fluently. He also has a degree in civil engineering. I'm pretty sure he knows that's a glass of water."

Liam, I'm chuckling to myself now as I write this, but earlier tonight I wanted to crawl under a rock. I was embarrassed as all get-out for Agnes and mortified for Fakhir. After finally realizing her faux pas (or fux pux, as you like to say) Agnes made a quick exit, and thankfully Fakhir found the whole episode amusing. (I guess he's used to that sort of thing by now, having been in the States almost two months already.) We ended up having a good laugh over it, which was a nice way to conclude our first evening together after all.

Thursday, January 31, 2008   6:19 p.m.

I got your email saying you left Camp Pendleton yesterday and stopped in Bangor, Maine early this morning to refuel. I feel terrible—the last time we spoke on the phone it was mostly about me and the boys and barely anything about you. You probably couldn't say much about your travel plans anyway but still, I feel bad. I should've known that might be your final phone call from inside the U.S. My only consolation is knowing the last thing we said to each other before we hung up was I love you.

How comforting it must have been for you and your fellow Marines when you got off the plane in Bangor to be met by the Maine Troop Greeters. That they would leave their homes to come to the airport, anytime of day—even in the middle of the night—to offer you guys handshakes and snacks, well, it just makes me want to lay my head down and cry with gratitude.

I'm anxiously awaiting word of when you've arrived at your next stop. I understand it could take several days to get to your final destination, and you may not have access to a phone or computer along the way.

Everything here is fine, and I'm not just saying that. It really is. We all love you more than ever.

Friday, February 1, 2008 10:23 p.m.

I got the note you sent from the USO computer, saying you made it as far as Kuwait and next you'll be moving into Iraq. I know you were anxious to move forward with this deployment, and even though the long days and nights of traveling have got to be grueling, in some ways it must be satisfying to finally land overseas and get on with the mission. I'm looking forward to hearing more of what the journey has been like so far.

Unlike the dusty conditions in Kuwait, we had an ice storm here last night. It was super windy, and as I was leaving for work this morning I noticed several shingles had blown off our roof. My plan was to call someone to replace the shingles while I was at work today but unfortunately I didn't have a spare moment.

So when I pulled in the driveway after work and saw Fakhir up on our roof hammering shingles, I felt a mixture of relief, amusement, and alarm. I quickly parked the car in the garage and returned to stand in the middle of the driveway where I could see him.

"You're gonna break a leg up there," I call out.

He stops hammering for a moment and waves. "Did you say something?"

"That roof is covered in ice," I shout. "I'm afraid you'll slide off and break a leg!"

"I'm fine," he shouts back, tugging at the rope he's got tied around his waist. I follow the line of the rope and see he's got the other end wrapped securely around the chimney. Fakhir smiles broadly, as if he's actually enjoying himself up there. Somehow this doesn't surprise me, knowing he spent the last three years hanging out with the likes of you and Wade Miller. I mean, who else thinks rappelling out of a perfectly good helicopter is not only an important life skill, but a fun way to pass the time?

I'm about to go inside when Vince comes out of their house to see if we need any help. Fakhir is just finishing up so he tells us he's got it and prepares to come down. Vince and I watch silently, fascinated, as Fakhir expertly rappels down the front of our house.

"Wow!" Vince exclaims as Fakhir lands in front of us. "That's impressive."

Fakhir unties the rope around his waist, smiles at Vince and says, "Thanks."

I jump in to make introductions. "Fakhir, this is our neighbor Vince. He's married to Wanda, who I'm sure you'll meet very soon. Vince, this is Fakhir."

Fakhir removes one of his work gloves and reaches out to shake Vince's hand. "Nice to meet you."

Vince returns Fakhir's handshake with enthusiasm. "Welcome to the neighborhood," he says.

The two of them start chatting about how to rappel off a cliff and what type of equipment works best. Meanwhile I'm freezing my ass off, already picturing mini-marshmallows gently bobbing on the surface of the steaming hot chocolate I plan to make as soon as I'm in the house. I politely excuse myself, leaving Vince and Fakhir to stand outside in the numbing cold. The last thing I hear before closing the door is Fakhir offering to take Vince rappelling. Wanda's going to love that.

And here I thought Vince was your typical garden-variety orthodontist. Who knew he had a rugged outdoorsmen hiding inside, waiting for someone like Fakhir to come along and set him free?

Things with Fakhir are falling into place. He has his room arranged the way he likes it, everything neat and tidy. I told him he should keep the door closed so the animals don't get pet hair all over his stuff. (He still doesn't appear too comfortable with them yet, which is another reason I suggested he keep his door closed. But I didn't tell him that.) Brig still barks at him every time he goes from one room to the next, and Soda continues to growl anytime Fakhir so much as looks at him. I hope the dogs get over themselves. Fakhir tries to be a good sport about the whole thing but I think Soda and Brig are hurting his feelings.

He doesn't seem too crazy about the cats either — which of course means they are highly interested in him. Last night Fakhir sat down to watch some TV with us and the cats were all over him. Daly wound herself around his ankles, Smedley jumped on his lap to make biscuits, and Button perched on his shoulder to lick the side of his face. Fakhir's like, "Umm, are these guys planning to hurt me?" The boys and I laughed and assured Fakhir the cats won't hurt him — in fact it seems they kind of like him. Nonetheless I shooed all three cats away but they kept coming back. It's as if they know Fakhir's not a cat person and they're hell-bent on ambushing him with affection every time he sits down.

Be safe, and take a lot of pictures if you can. Know that I'm thinking of you every minute, wondering what you're doing and what it's like for you. The boys miss you too but we're all focusing on getting through the day and staying positive. I'll call your mom to let her know you arrived in the Middle East.

Your dad would be so proud of you.

Saturday, February 2, 2008   10:17 a.m.

Col. Phillips called from the base early this morning to say you made it safely into Baghdad. After I got off the phone with him I ran to the computer to check my email and sure enough there was a note from you saying as much. I'm so happy to hear from you and to know you're OK. I wasn't expecting to hear anything until tomorrow at the earliest. I'll make this short so you get a response before you turn in for the night, and you can go to sleep tonight knowing we know you're safe.

All my love.

10:39 a.m.

Dear Friends & Family:

I received an email from Liam saying he arrived safely in Baghdad. When we last spoke with him Monday night he was still in California. After he left Camp Pendleton they weren't allowed to call anyone en route, and we didn't know how many days it would take for him to get to his final stop. So we were relieved and happy to finally hear from him. He wrote from the email account of the guy he's replacing, who's giving him a tour of the base tonight. He's been assigned temporary quarters and I hope he'll be able to get a good night's rest. They're nine hours ahead in Baghdad. I know many of you have had Liam in your thoughts, and would be happy to hear of his safe arrival.

Emilie

8:24 p.m.

Liam, I sent a note to family and friends letting them know you're in Baghdad now. I've been getting lots of phone calls and emails lately, mostly from friends and family back home wondering how you're doing. I hope they don't mind getting status updates via mass email. It's just easier that way. I did spend some time this afternoon returning calls. A few people have invited me out for coffee or a movie. I truly appreciate when someone reaches out to me like that. But (other than book club) I don't feel like socializing much right now. I know everyone says it's good to get out at times like this, but solitude is what heals me.

Sunday, February 3, 2008   6:46 p.m.

I can't tell you how reassuring it was to hear your voice this morning. I don't know how we survived previous deployments without phone calls and email. Remember when Rory was a baby and you deployed to Colombia for three months? You were only allowed to call home once the entire time you were gone. We didn't even know where you were, what you were doing, or when you'd be back. And how about all those exercises in South Korea when we were first married? Our only communication was through handwritten letters. And yet, we managed — just like all the military families who went before us.

It's too bad we couldn't talk longer, but I understand you had to keep it short. I'm just glad you were able to get through, since you said Sunday nights (Baghdad time) are when everyone tries to call home and it's hard to get a line out.

After we spoke I ran to Target and bought you an iHome for your iPod so you can listen to music in your CHU. (Couldn't they come up with something a little more snappy than "Containerized Housing Unit"?) At least you have a decent place to lay your head at night. I hope it's safe.

I'll take the iHome to the post office on my lunch break tomorrow, along with more photos of the family as requested, and the non-liquid, non-aerosol room freshener you asked for. Does your CHU smell bad or something? Or maybe it's for your office? Oh, and don't worry about the restrictions — I wasn't planning on sending you any pork or porn anyway. Though I'm told other wives do it. (Send nudes, that is. Unless you'd rather have bacon?)

Since it's already the middle of the night (or early Monday morning) where you are, I wonder if you were able to stay awake to watch the Super Bowl? Or did you go to sleep and set your alarm for 2:30 a.m.? It's great you guys can see sporting events in real time these days. Remember when we were stationed on Okinawa in the '80s, and FEN broadcast the previous year's Super Bowl game because they couldn't get a feed of the live game? It was so dumb because we already knew the outcome — but we had a Super Bowl party anyway! And it was fun.

Speaking of which, Rory and Fakhir are in the basement watching the game as I write this. (Finn is out getting his hair cut by a friend. I know he's supposed to be grounded. I let him out for just this one thing.)

Funny story: At breakfast this morning Fakhir asked Rory if he wanted to watch the "Super Ball" with him later. Rory's like, "Super Ball? What are you talking about dude?" And Fakhir says, "You know, the big football game you Americans make such a huge deal about every year. The

Super Ball." Rory says, "You mean the Super *Bowl*?" and Fakhir's like, "Yeah. That's what I said."

Fakhir's English is flawless. But sometimes he comes out with these little zingers. Funny thing is, when he mixes something up like that, it actually makes more sense the way *he* says it. Did he do that a lot when you guys served together?

Rory and Fakhir have hit it off quite nicely. Fakhir promised to watch the game with Rory if Rory agreed to finish his homework first. (I love not having to be the official nagger around here all the time!) As for myself, I'm upstairs watching the Puppy Bowl on Animal Planet, snuggled in bed with my laptop and surrounded by the pets. The cats don't seem to care much, but Soda and Brig can't take their eyes off the TV screen.

Monday, February 4, 2008   10:06 p.m.

FYSA: Finn dyed his hair blue.

(If you're reading this far, I imagine you have now picked yourself up off the floor and are once again seated in front of your computer.)

Here's how it went down. Finn knows a girl at school who supposedly works in a hair salon, and she offered to do his hair for free at her house. As I explained in my email last night, I know he's supposed to be grounded. But he worked extra-long hours at the coffee shop this weekend. And my heart softened when he asked if he could go do this hair appointment thing after dinner last night — especially since I knew he wasn't interested in watching the "Super Ball." It wasn't like he was asking to go to a party or anything. I mean, how much trouble could a guy get into going to a girl's house to get his hair done? (He did mention something about "changing up" his hairstyle when he left the house, but I took that to mean a new haircut.)

He comes home a few hours later with bright blue hair. I was straightening up the kitchen and luckily I wasn't holding anything breakable or I might've dropped it. You would've been proud of me though — before I got all wound up over his blue hair (did I mention it's really bright?) I asked myself: "Is this something that will affect his life ten years from now?" And, since the answer is no, I was able to get my wits about me and act remarkably nonchalant. (Which was something of a surprise to Finn — from the nervous look on his face I think he was anticipating some fireworks.)

"That's a new look," I say.

He stands hesitantly at the entrance to the kitchen. "Do you ... like it?" he asks.

I think on it a few seconds. It actually does look kinda good on him. "It goes well with your blue eyes," I tell him.

"Thanks," he replies, his shoulders relaxing.

I return to wiping down the countertops, silently going over the calendar in my head to make sure his hair will grow out in time for graduation.

Meanwhile Fakhir comes upstairs from the basement and stops in his tracks when he sees Finn's hair. He utters a little "Oh," and immediately looks at me in order to get a read on what I'm thinking about this new development.

I shrug and give him the "What's a mother to do?" look. (We've had a few of these visual exchanges lately while he figures out how things work around here).

Once he gathers I'm not upset (at least not visibly), Fakhir smiles and pats Finn on the back. "Nice job bro. At least you were smart enough to wait until your dad is almost seven thousand miles away."

Finn grins back, rubbing a hand over his newly blue hair. "Thanks. That's pretty much what I was thinking."

Meanwhile Rory strolls into the kitchen for a glass of milk. He walks right past Finn and opens the fridge door. With his back to us, he says to Finn, "Does Dad know you did that?"

Photo of Finn's new hair attached. (Did I mention it's really blue?)

Tuesday, February 5, 2008   9:08 p.m.

I was happy to see your email before I left for work this morning. Thank God you still have your sense of humor. And I'm glad you sent Finn a note telling him you're not upset about his hair. (Don't worry, I won't tell anyone what a softie you are.)

It's good there haven't been any increased threat alerts since you got there. I'm still scanning the newspaper and watching the news every night for any reports from Baghdad. Still, are you getting used to wearing a pistol to work every day again? You said you've been able to go running on base a few times — is your route well-protected? I know you won't have to wear the full combat gear unless you're moving between bases but how often will that be?

You'd think after almost 25 years of marriage I'd be used to the questions some people ask me about your deployments. (Seems to go from one extreme to the other — either people ignore me entirely or the ones who do ask questions make me want to stab myself in the neck with a pencil.)

I was on my break in the lunchroom today and one woman in particular asks me questions about your deployment every single time we run into each other. It doesn't matter if we're in the hallway, the lunchroom, the mailroom, or even the bathroom. We can't just exchange pleasant hellos. No. There has to be some type of in-depth, serious conversation about The War. (I mean, I appreciate her concern and all, but some days I'm just not up to playing Twenty Questions about you being in a combat zone. One of the reasons I took this job was so I wouldn't be sitting at home consumed with worry every minute of every day.)

So anyways I sit down at a conference table in the lunchroom, purposely seating myself at the far end of the table from Tiffany. The polite side of me wants to smile and say hello but the jerk side of me wants to pretend she doesn't exist for fear of her starting up yet another War Conversation. As I'm staring intently at the contents of my lunch cooler (PBJ, chips & an orange) I can feel her eyes on me. The polite side of me can't take it any longer so I glance in her direction, smile, and say hello.

"Hey!" she says. "How ya doin'? Are you worried about your husband now that he's in the sandbox?"

Oh great. Now she sounds like she's been brushing up on her war lingo in between How To Be An Asshole seminars.

"Well, yes, of course I'm worried about him you fucking idiot. Thank you for reminding me of my deepest fucking fears every single fucking time I venture outside my fucking classroom." That's what the jerk side of me *wants* to say but I manage to keep it in check. Instead I reply, "Yes, I'm very worried about him. But he's doing okay at the moment. Thank you for asking."

She pops a tater tot into her mouth and says, "So. Whatcha been doing to keep yourself busy since he's been gone?"

I'm about to take a bite of my PBJ but I set it back down instead. "Well, let's see … You mean other than working, raising two teenage boys, paying bills, doing laundry, grocery shopping, cooking, and watching the house clean itself you goddamn motherfucking moron?" No, I don't say that either. That would be the jerk side of me talking. The polite side of me says, "Oh, this and that. We stay pretty busy."

By this time I'm glancing up at the clock on the wall, thinking it's time for my break to be over (even if it's not). I put my uneaten sandwich back in the Ziploc baggie and place it in the cooler. Yet before I can make my getaway, she leans forward confidingly and says, "I can relate to what you're going through. Last month, my boyfriend left for two whole weeks on a business trip to Cleveland. I literally thought I was going to lose my mind!"

"Really?" I look at her, wide-eyed, shaking my head. "I hadn't heard about the mortar attacks in Ohio." That is actually me talking. It appears my jerk side has temporarily wrested control of my mouth from the polite side.

Tiffany stares at me blankly, then pops three tater tots into her mouth at once, chewing in silence. I'm not sure if she doesn't know what to say or doesn't know what a mortar is. (Time to do some more brushing up on her war lingo I guess.)

I tell Tiffany I just remembered something I had to finish before fifth hour. I grab my lunch and bolt out of the room before she can say anything else and my body becomes completely possessed by the jerk side.

Walking back to my classroom I take deep calming breaths. I tell myself I should be grateful when people show an interest in our family and in what you're doing over there. Wasn't it just a few weekends ago I was complaining because no one was asking me about you? The polite side of me vows to be more gracious in the future. Perhaps I'm just feeling a little raw since it wasn't that long ago you left. (Or maybe I'll feel this way the entire twelve months you're gone?)

I realize people are coming from a place of kindness when they ask questions like Tiffany was just asking. I know she didn't mean any harm, and that her intention was to be supportive and friendly. People like her are just trying to connect and show they care. Most people have no idea what it's like to be part of a military family, and it's hard for them to know what to say in times like this. So they say whatever comes to mind, in an effort to reach out.

I'm going to try harder to keep that in mind in the future. And if someone I don't know well starts asking me things I don't want to talk about, I'll tactfully change the subject to something like books or movies or TV shows or even the weather. I've never been very good at small talk, but it's time I get better at it. Because that kind of normal chitchat is what keeps us from collapsing under the weight of a long deployment. If I let my worries take front and center every hour of every day you're gone, I wouldn't be able to function.

I unlock the door of my classroom, sit down at my desk, and restart my computer. I should look on the bright side, I think. At least Tiffany refrained from offering me her political opinions about our military presence in Iraq. (That's always a fun conversation.) Or asking me if I'm afraid you're going to come home and go crazy and try to kill me in my sleep or something.

You're not, are you?

Wednesday, February 6, 2008   8:30 p.m.

Thanks for the reassurances about your running route, and the description of your work routine so far. I can see why everyone works 12-hour days, seven days a week over there, since there's not much else to do anyway. Still, at some point it would begin to feel like Groundhog Day if you don't do something different once in a while.

How are you able to get a good night's sleep with a gigantic generator running right outside your CHU and trucks driving by all night? Isn't that going to damage your hearing after a while? I don't suppose earplugs are an option. Sleeping through an incoming mortar siren probably wouldn't be a very good idea.

You must be exhausted, what with the time difference plus getting used to strange surroundings and learning the new job. Sounds like you have a lot to learn before the guy you're replacing leaves next week. Just think, less than a year from now you'll be the one briefing your replacement.

Agnes called tonight to ask if Ethan could stay at our house this weekend while she and Eugene are out of town. I told her Rory has a hockey game Saturday night but Ethan's welcome to stay here as long as he doesn't mind going to the game with us. I know Rory and Ethan are friends but nonetheless I was surprised Agnes didn't ask someone else to watch Ethan, what with you being gone and everything we have going on right now. But then again she's another one who thinks I'm sitting around all day eating bon bons since you left. (She probably thinks she's doing me a favor by tasking me with something to keep me busy. Ha!) In any case, I'm sure Ethan will be no trouble.

Did I tell you Finn and his friends are starting a band? They asked if they could practice in the garage this weekend and crazy me said yes. Neil is lead singer and lead guitarist, Crystal is bass player and backup singer, Daryll is on drums, and Finn will play keyboards. Who knows if anything will come of it. At the very least they'll have some fun. And it'll be good practice for Finn while he waits to hear about financial aid from the music schools he applied to. (By the way, Finn has yet to finish filling out his FAFSA. I don't think the colleges will finalize his scholarships until they get that form. Another thing I've been nagging about lately.)

Fakhir had a meeting on base yesterday with his future bosses. The plan was to finalize a start date for his job working as a contractor with the military. When he first came here they told him he'd be starting soon. Unfortunately yesterday they gave him some disappointing news: It could be another few months for his security clearance to go through. Which means it'll be at least that long before he can start the new job. I don't understand why they have to do a background investigation all over again—I'm sure they did one when he was working with our troops in Iraq, right? Can't they just renew the security clearance he had before? Or do they have stricter protocols now that he's in the U.S.? (He also told me the other night he wants to apply to become a U.S. citizen, but he has to be here a while longer before he can start the paperwork.)

Keeping in mind what Fakhir learned about the job on base yesterday, let me tell you what happened this afternoon. I'm driving home from work when I get a call on my cell from the manager at the McDonald's a mile from our house. He asks me to verify Fakhir's work history and if he is who he says he is, which I confirm. After I hang up from that guy I call Fakhir on his cell. "Fakhir, did you just apply for a job at McDonald's?" and he says, "Yeah, I hope you don't mind I gave your name as a reference." I tell him that's fine but there's no need for him to work while he's waiting for the military job; he can stay with us as long as he needs to, blah blah blah blah blah. Meanwhile Fakhir's getting another call so he hangs up with me to answer it. I arrive back home a few minutes later to find Fakhir waiting for me in the kitchen. He informs me he got the job at McDonald's and he starts work in the morning! Can you believe it?

As Fakhir tells it, after I left for work this morning he walked up to the main drag, filled out an application at McDonald's and had an interview on the spot. "Why McDonald's?" I ask. He says one of his favorite movies as a kid was "Coming to America" with Eddie Murphy. And that he always thought, if he couldn't get an engineering job in the U.S., it would be fun to work at a hamburger place like the one in the movie.

Thursday, February 7, 2008   8:08 p.m.

Your idea to tell Finn he can't hold band practice in the garage until he sends in his FAFSA was brilliant. After I saw your email I told Finn that was the deal and, sure enough, he finished the form and sent it in after school today. Thanks! You're smarter than you look.

Fakhir's first day at McDonald's went well. He said he spent most of the day in training, going over the employee handbook, and filling out various forms. Before the dinner rush started, the manager put Fakhir on the register, and he was impressed with how quickly Fakhir picked up on taking orders and making change. (I mean, he is an engineer after all.) So they gave him his uniform and told him to show up for the breakfast shift tomorrow morning.

In other news, the toilet off the kitchen was making weird noises when I came home from work, and no one else was home yet to help me figure out what was wrong with it. However, I'm pleased to inform you I fixed it. All by myself. Here's what I did: I pulled on the thingie with the chain which lifted the other thingie and caused the water in the tank to drain. Then I let go of the first thingie and made sure the other thingie looked like it was where it's supposed to be. It stopped making the funny noises so I'm positive I fixed it. I guess we'll know for sure if we don't get woken up in the middle of the night by an exploding toilet.

In the three and a half weeks since you left, the garage door motor went AWOL, a shit ton of shingles blew off the roof, the ice machine went on the fritz, the fan in the basement bathroom started making sounds like a jet ready for takeoff, and today the powder room toilet was on permanent flush. There's a reason it's called the Deployment Curse.

I suppose it could also have something to do with this house being 80 years old. I mean, I love our tree-lined neighborhood and quiet cul-de-sac. But sometimes I wonder if we should've bought a house with a little less "character."

Don't get me wrong—I'm glad we decided to live off base this tour. (Well, except for that one time before the Turnabout Dance a few weekends ago.) I mean, the whole idea was to give Finn and Rory a chance to experience life outside the gates, right? Especially now that they're in high school. It was time for them to spread their wings, make friends with kids whose parents aren't in the military, and get a taste of what life is like on the civilian side.

We did have some good times living on base at our other duty stations though. Being surrounded by other military families does have its perks—like a built-in support network during deployments. The other thing I miss is the sense of security that comes with living on a military base. And it sure was nice being so close to the commissary and PX. That said, I think we made the right decision to live off base this time, don't you?

Friday, February 8, 2008   5:44 p.m.

I just finished quizzing Fakhir on the menu items at McDonald's. Poor guy. I guess his first day working the front counter didn't go so well. They threw him right into the fire and put him on the cash register first thing this morning. He's a smart guy; he probably would've been fine if it wasn't the breakfast shift.

As Fakhir explained it when I got home from work this afternoon, "I get the hamburger part. I get the chicken sandwich, the fish filet, the French fries — all of that. But the breakfast items — Egg McMuffin? What is that? In Iraq we serve breakfast on a platter. We have eggs. We have pastries. We have a lot of the same things you have here in the U.S. But we don't serve breakfast on a sandwich. We put it on a plate."

So here he is, working the register when the place opens, and people are ordering Sausage McGriddles and Bacon Egg & Cheese Biscuits and whatnot, and he has no idea what the hell they're talking about. He didn't grow up eating McDonald's, and he most certainly had never eaten breakfast at a McDonald's. And it's not like knowing the difference between a muffin and a biscuit and a bagel is information that comes in handy on the battlefield. (Or that a McGriddle is a sandwich made out of two pancakes — even I didn't know that. Who thinks up this shit?)

He told me he muddled his way through the shift with the help of his coworkers, and that the manager didn't seem too concerned. But Fakhir was upset with himself for being unprepared. After the shift was over he went to the manager's office and asked if he could take home a training manual listing all the menu items. And now he's sitting at the kitchen table studying that thing. I told him he's being too hard on himself, yet I have no doubt come morning he'll know that manual backwards and forwards.

Rory brought Ethan home from school with him today. Ethan is a pleasant enough young man. (Kind of a suck-up actually — I had put on sweats and a t-shirt as soon as I got home from work and he tells me how nice I look. Rrrriiiight.)

In case you forgot, Ethan is spending the weekend with us while Agnes and Eugene are out of town. Agnes showed up at our door last night with a huge bag of special food for Ethan: soy milk, goji berries, Swiss chard, dried plums, and quinoa. It's not like Ethan has allergies or anything. I hope she doesn't expect me to whip up some kind of special meal for him while he's here? (In fact, I just ordered an extra-large pizza from Peroni's before I sat down to write this email.) And what the hell are goji berries anyway? I tried feeding some to Soda and Brig but even they weren't interested.

Neil, Crystal, and Darryl are coming over after dinner for the inaugural band practice. Finn is out in the garage right now setting up the space heater. It's 11° outside but no way in hell am I letting those kids hold band practice inside the house. They'll be fine in the garage. I just hope the neighbors don't complain.

Gotta run — pizza should be here any minute.

p.s. Do you get pizza in the DFAC?

Saturday, February 9, 2008   10:17 a.m.

I'm glad you find my Fakhir stories amusing. Having him here has been our good fortune. And he thinks we're the ones doing him a favor.

It's nice they let you have near-beers once in a while since alcohol isn't allowed. Why am I not surprised you went to the trouble of calculating you'd have to drink 72 near-beers to get the alcoholic equivalent of a six-pack? (And please don't tell me you actually attempted this.)

Speaking of beer, we're having another fun-filled weekend here at the Mahoney house. This time it's Rory who wins the Dilliclapper of the Month award.

After we finished dinner last night — no, wait. Let me back up a little, to when we first sat down to dinner. We'd all just taken our seats around the table. It's me, Fakhir, Finn, Rory, and Ethan. Everyone's excited about the extra-large veggie pizza that had just been delivered. Except before we open the box and start eating, Ethan notices the empty place setting in the spot where you usually sit.

"Is someone else coming for dinner?" he asks, eyeing the extra plate.

"That's my dad's spot," Rory says.

Ethan looks around the table uncertainly. "Your dad is coming home from Iraq for dinner?"

"No, douche pickle," Finn says. "He can't just fly back for dinner."

"Finn be nice," I warn.

"That's their way of honoring their dad while he's gone," Fakhir jumps in to explain. "It's ... a symbol. It means he won't be forgotten. And that his place at the table will be waiting for him when he comes back."

"Wow," Ethan marvels. "That is so touching. Your dad is such a hero." As if on cue his chest heaves theatrically. He grabs his napkin off the table and uses it to dab at the corner of his eye.

Finn lets his head fall back, mouth open, exhaling loudly in disbelief. He then quickly snaps his head forward to look at Ethan. "Dude. For real? You don't need to fake cry for us. We're fine."

"Finn! That's not very nice," I say. And yet I can't keep the corners of my mouth from curling into the tiniest hint of a smile. Finn and I exchange knowing looks. We're onto the Eddie Haskell routine.

"Can we stop talking and just eat?" Rory asks, reaching for the pizza box and flipping it open. "I'm starving."

Fast-forward to when we're done with dinner, but still sitting around the table. Rory asks if he and Ethan can ride their bikes up to Jack in the Box.

"Why do you need to go to Jack in the Box?" I ask. "We just ate."

Rory shrugs. "It's where all the freshman from school go. We don't get food — we just hang out in the parking lot."

"We?"

Rory's face immediately turns red as he realizes his mistake.

"Busted!" Finn calls out with glee.

"Shut your pie-hole!" Rory shoots back.

"Boys, knock it off," I say. "Rory, you know the drill. You're supposed to keep me posted of your whereabouts at all times. This Jack in the Box business is news to me."

"I know. I'm sorry Mom. It was just like, one or two times."

Ethan stares down at his empty plate and quietly snorts.

"Is there something amusing you'd like to share with us Ethan?" I ask.

"No, ma'am." He raises his eyes from his plate and presents me with a carefully crafted look of wide-eyed innocence.

Fakhir, meanwhile, watches the conversation unfold with interest. He catches my eye and raises an eyebrow at Ethan's latest performance.

I turn my attention back to Rory. "On top of everything else, it's freezing out and there's snow on the ground. Riding your bikes up to Jack in the Box and standing outside in the parking lot doesn't even sound fun. Why don't you two stay inside and watch a movie?"

"Because everyone in the universe is hanging out at Jack in the Box tonight," he pleads. "And besides, Mom, it's only a few blocks away and the streets have been plowed."

I don't know what's gotten into me since you left. I'm the one who's the strict disciplinarian around here. But lately I find myself saying yes to things I'd never let the boys do if you were here. Against my better judgment I say, "Okay. You can go. Only because you're being honest this time by asking my permission beforehand. I expect you back home by ten o'clock on the dot. Both of you." I punctuate this last part with a cautionary look in Ethan's direction.

"Thank you Mrs. Mahoney," Ethan says as he and Rory get up from the table to take their plates to the sink. "You're the absolute best mom in the whole neighborhood."

Fakhir and I roll our eyes at each other while Finn appears to have a coughing fit, except we can hear him muttering "horseshit" in between coughs.

Rory returns from the sink to give me a kiss before he and Ethan head out the door. "Thanks Mom."

Once the table is cleared and Finn and friends have started up with their band practice, Fakhir and I devise a plan. (By the way, did you happen to leave any of your earplugs from the shooting range at home?

I don't mean to insult the kids' musical talents, but the term "ear-splitting" comes to mind.). Anyhow. Getting back to our plan. Stealth mom that I am, I suggest going on a little recon mission to make sure Rory and Ethan actually are at Jack in the Box like they said they'd be. I also want to make sure they're not getting themselves into any sort of trouble. Fakhir eagerly agrees to join me.

We hop in the car and, within minutes, we're slowly cruising past the Jack in the Box. "Can you see anything?" I ask Fakhir, who's crouched in the passenger seat scanning the parking lot through a pair of binoculars.

"I have visual contact on Ethan and Rory," he says.

"Excellent. What else do you see?"

"Nothing really," he says. "What am I looking for?"

"I don't know," I reply. "Anything suspicious."

I make a U-turn so we can do another drive-by. "What do you see this time?" I ask.

"Just a bunch of kids standing around with their hands in their pockets trying to look like they're not freezing their asses off," he says.

I pull into the CVS parking lot next door to Jack in the Box. "Here, let me take a look," I say, grabbing the binoculars from Fakhir.

I scrunch down in the driver's seat and have a look. The situation is exactly as Fakhir described: A group of about a dozen kids, who appear to be comporting themselves in a manner expected of most 14-year olds. That is to say, they're standing around trying to act cool. Nothing unsavory appears to be going on.

Fakhir and I head home.

As it turns out, our recon mission hadn't been as thorough as we thought. What we didn't see when we drove by was that the kids apparently had multiple cans of beer hidden in their jacket pockets and underneath their hoodies. (Had we seen that, I assure you Fakhir and I would have gotten out of the car and un-assed every single one of those kids before calling their parents to come pick them up.)

We didn't learn what had been going on until Ethan and Rory walk in the door at ten o'clock smelling like a brewery. (Hey, at least they were on time, right? I suppose they thought we wouldn't notice they were slightly inebriated as long as they met their curfew. Wrong.)

First thing they do when they step foot inside the foyer is call out, "Hey, we're home." Fakhir and I are in the family room watching TV. (Or, trying to watch TV. Finn et al. are still making a racket in the garage.) From where I'm sitting I can see they're having a bit of trouble hanging up their coats in the hall closet — fumbling around and giggling like a couple of schoolgirls.

Next thing that happens is they attempt to make a beeline upstairs without coming into the family room to tell me about their night as per our house rules. Big mistake.

Before they can get all the way up the stairs, I call out (loud enough to be heard above the music — if that's what you wanna call it), " Boys."

I can see their feet through the railing. They freeze mid-step. "Yeah?" Rory calls back.

"Come here and say hello to Fakhir and me."

Two sets of feet turn toward each other in what I imagine to be a confab of urgent whispering. Shortly thereafter they're standing reluctantly before us in the family room. Ethan is wearing the fakest smile I've ever seen. (He must be taking lessons from his mother.)

"So. How was your night?" I ask.

They both nod energetically. "Good." "It was great."

"Come closer where I can get a better look at you two."

They take a cautious step forward. Fakhir and I breathe deeply. The room smells like the bottom of a can of Pabst Blue Ribbon.

"How many beers did each of you drink tonight?" I ask.

"Mrs. Mahoney! I'm underage. I would never break the law." Ethan looks absolutely shocked and appalled that I would even suggest such a thing. If I didn't know better I might almost have second thoughts about accusing him of drinking. Almost.

Rory, for his part, remains silent. At least he knows better than to lie or argue with me. (Perhaps he was eavesdropping on my little chat with Finn last month. Lesson learned: Don't bullshit Mom.)

I observe the boys without saying anything, tapping my fingers on my thigh while I think. Fakhir uses the remote to turn down the volume on the TV.

Ethan makes another attempt at defending himself. "Scout's honor Mrs. Mahoney — "

I cut him down at the knees. "Zip it, LCpl. Schmuckatelli. I've had enough of you." I shift my gaze between the two boys. "You are *both* in deep shit. You might have only had two or three beers, but that is two or three beers too many for 14-year-old boys. Rory, you're grounded until further notice. Ethan, I have no choice but to tell your mom about this when she comes to pick you up Sunday morning."

This time Ethan looks like he really is going to cry.

"I want both of you to go directly upstairs, put on your pajamas, and hit the rack. Lights out. No talking. Now pop smoke."

The two young hooligans can't get up the stairs fast enough.

Damn. I was hoping we'd at least get Finn off to college before Rory commenced with the high school shenanigans. But don't you fret. I can handle Rory. The fun part is going to be when Agnes comes to pick up Ethan tomorrow and hears her little angel is not so angelic after all. Now that's going to be a soup sandwich!

Sunday, February 10, 2008   7:22 p.m.

Thanks for the email. You must've been up early. I wish we could've spoken on the phone this morning, but if Gen. Petraeus wants to hold a VTC I guess you can't very well tell him you have a phone date with your wife.

The conversation with Agnes when she came to pick up Ethan earlier today was, as expected, unpleasant. I went out of my way to be matter-of-fact about it, and to emphasize it was both of the boys who had misbehaved. I didn't want her to think I was being judgmental or singling out Ethan.

But alas, from the look she gave me she might as well have told me to go pound sand, fuck you very much. What's worse, instead of taking my word for it, she stood there questioning me, like how did I know they'd been drinking, and did I have any proof? I told her they both smelled like alcohol and it was obvious from their behavior they'd been drinking. I'm trying to stay calm but the more she questions me the more pissed I'm getting. Because the last thing I need to be doing right now is defending myself to another parent — especially in front of the boys.

She didn't even bother to thank me for keeping Ethan all weekend. All she said before she and Ethan left was that she'd discuss it with him when they got home and she'd get back to me. Well, I don't give a rat's ass if she gets back to me or not. As far as I'm concerned, case closed — end of story, fuckity bye.

Oh, and I also gave her back the huge bag of special foods Ethan didn't touch the whole time he was here because he was too busy stuffing his face with Cheese Puffs and Sour Patch Kids. (I didn't tell her that, but I did seriously consider telling her to take her damn Swiss chard and shove it up her ass.)

About an hour after they left, the phone rings and it's Agnes. She tells me she spoke with Ethan and he swears up and down he hadn't been drinking; he said he only smelled like alcohol because Rory was the one drinking and Rory spilled beer on Ethan's jeans. And she believes him. The little shit. (I did ask Rory if this was true and he said no, they'd both been drinking. Plus, I saw it with my very own eyes — Ethan was liquored up!) Whatever. I told Agnes it's between her and Ethan now and I had nothing further to say on the matter.

After that conversation I needed some stress relief so I grabbed the car keys and wandered around Target for a couple hours. What is it about that place that's so relaxing? Do you think they pump Xanax through the air vents or something? I get myself a venti vanilla latte and push the red cart up and down the aisles, looking at a bunch of crap I didn't realize we needed until I see it on the shelves at Target. Like this little coffee creamer thingie shaped like a cow where the cream comes out of the cow's mouth. (Yeah I bought it.) And matching Argyle sweaters for the dogs. (OK yeah I bought those too.) And how about boxer shorts with little red hearts for the boys? (Yep, got those.) But I resisted the more high-ticket items like an animal-print area rug for the family room and a lamp shaped like the Eiffel tower. All in all, a relatively inexpensive therapy session.

When I got home there was a message from Wade Miller inviting me out to dinner with him and Isabel and Chloe on Valentine's Day. How nice is that? But instead of tagging along with them, I think I'll call him back and offer to watch the baby while they go out and have a date by themselves. Wade mentioned when he was here for dinner a couple weeks ago that things have been a little rocky between him and Isabel lately. It'll be good for them to have some alone time, don't you think?

Speaking of Valentines, will you be mine?

Monday, February 11, 2008

The Midwest Courier Times
<u>International News</u>, page 14

U.S. colonel killed in Iraq

Washington DC—According to an anonymous source with ties to the Defense Department, a U.S. colonel was killed during a mortar attack yesterday in Baghdad. The colonel was stationed on Camp Victory working for the Multi-National Force-Iraq and was reportedly jogging inside the perimeter when he was struck by indirect mortar fire. According to the source, who spoke on condition of anonymity, U.S. Forces have experienced a recent upsurge in violence surrounding the Victory Base Complex (VBC). It is not yet known if there were other casualties related to this incident. Colonel appears to be the highest rank of any U.S. military deaths during Operation Iraqi Freedom. According to an Associated Press database, at least eight other colonels have died in Iraq. The officer's name has not been released pending notification of family.

5:03 p.m.

Liam,

I read in the paper after getting home from work today that a colonel on Camp Victory has been killed. My head tells me it's not you, because if it was, I would have been contacted by now, right? (Even though the article says the family has yet to be notified — goddamned "anonymous sources.") By my calculations, the paper would have been printed 15 hours ago — surely enough time for the family to have been informed, wouldn't you think?

But my heart ... my heart needs to be reassured. I've searched online but all I can find is the same AP news item being quoted by various news outlets. Please write back as soon as you can to tell me it's not you. I know it's not you. It can't be you. But the article said the colonel was jogging. It was just a small item in the back of the front section. Please. Tell me it wasn't you.

Emilie

10:23 p.m.

Liam, five hours may not be that long in ordinary circumstances. But we are not living an ordinary life right now, and the past five hours have been excruciating. I couldn't take it any longer so I finally picked up the phone and called Wade. He said he'd try to get a hold of Col. Phillips or the duty sergeant on base since it's after hours. Just to confirm that whoever was killed, it wasn't you. It's unthinkable I'd ever wish this fate on someone else's spouse, someone else's children. But please, let it be someone else. Not you.

Wade assured me they would've known something right away if it had been someone from the unit. And he told me I should get some rest while they get confirmation on that because it may take a while. But I won't rest — I can't rest — until I hear from you directly.

A snowstorm has begun and the school already announced a snow day for tomorrow. I didn't mention anything to the boys or even Fakhir about the item in the paper. And I made a point of not watching the news on TV like I usually do. (Luckily the boys don't share my habit of turning into a news junkie every time you go away.) I hid the newspaper, and after dinner I told everyone I wasn't feeling well. I came upstairs, closed the door, and laid on our bed holding my phone in one hand and hugging my laptop to my chest — thinking if I wish hard enough, an email or a phone call from you will come through.

Tuesday, February 12, 2008   2:04 a.m.

The most horrible thing just happened. I must have drifted off after I wrote you that last email. I was in a sound sleep when the doorbell rang. It seemed so loud, and I was frightened out of my mind. I bolted out of bed and flew down the stairs, certain I'd find a casualty officer on our doorstep. I flung open the door, my heart in my throat, only to find no one there. Nothing but the gathering snow and silence. I stood for a moment, my hand on my throat, trying to catch my breath and get a hold of myself. Then — laughter from the bushes on the side of the house and the sound of footsteps running away. Kids out late because of the snow day tomorrow. Having a sleepover probably, and, as kids are wont to do, snuck out to go ding dong ditching.

They had no way of knowing how upsetting it would be for a family like ours to hear a doorbell ringing in the middle of the night. They probably didn't notice or, more likely, didn't understand the meaning of the blue star flag in our front window. Half the grown-ups in town don't know what a blue star flag means — why would the kids be any different? Had they known, I'm sure they wouldn't have done it.

As I closed the door, Fakhir came up from the basement to see what was going on and the boys had come out of their bedrooms, standing sleepily on the landing to ask who rang the bell. I said everything is fine, just kids out fooling around, and told the boys to go back to bed. But Fakhir, who was standing in the foyer with me, could tell from the look on my face something was terribly wrong.

Once I was certain the boys were back in their rooms I got the newspaper out of the kitchen cabinet where I'd hidden it earlier, and showed the article to Fakhir. He said he'd stay up with me while I waited to hear from you or Wade or Col. Phillips but I said no, it wasn't necessary. He folded his arms and said there's no way he's going back to bed. That we could call the Red Cross if we hadn't heard anything by morning. We stood in the kitchen arguing with each other in lowered voices. I didn't tell Fakhir this, but I didn't want to cry in front of him. I wanted to be alone so I could cry in private. Instead I told him there's no sense in the both of us losing sleep. But he would have none of it. He convinced me to go upstairs and grab my laptop and cell phone so we could sit together in the family room and wait.

And that's where we are now, sitting in the dark so as not to disturb the boys. Waiting to hear from you. The cuckoo clock you brought home from Germany just struck two. Why haven't you answered my emails? Please. Let me know you're okay. That everything will be all right.

6:08 a.m.

Thank God you're all right. I'm sorry about all the fuss. I'm so embarrassed. Wade finally got a hold of Col. Phillips about five o'clock this morning and, as you now know, Ken patched a call through on the DSN line and left a message with someone there for you to call or email me. I feel like an idiot. I should have known you just didn't have time to check email. I can't begin to imagine how hectic — how horrible — the last 36 hours have been for you and everyone on Camp Victory. I'm sorry for adding to that stress. You had no way of knowing the incident involving the colonel you're replacing would make it into the papers so fast. And to think he was scheduled to rotate in just a few days.

I feel terrible knowing three Marines were killed in Sunday's mortar attack. And even more terrible for my overriding sense of relief that you weren't one of them.

Wednesday, February 13, 2008   9:07 p.m.

I confess to sleeping most of the day yesterday after having been up all night. And yes, I still feel like a jackass. But that's nothing compared to what you're going through. And the families of those who were killed. Were all three of the Marines stationed out of Twentynine Palms, or just the colonel you were replacing? I can't get it out of my mind how easily that could have been you, Liam. Will you at least stop jogging outdoors for a while?

Fakhir and I talked to Finn and Rory last night about what happened on Camp Victory. We figured they'd either see it on the news or some-one at school would ask them about it. I informed Fakhir ahead of time we are not telling them that one of the Marines who died was the guy you're replacing. They don't need to know that. We told them you're safe and that security on VBC has been stepped up.

Has the increased threat level changed any of your upcoming travel plans? I suppose you can't answer that. But if you *are* staying on base for the time being, can you at least tell me that much?

We ended up getting around six or seven inches of snow yesterday. It's the biggest snowfall Fakhir has seen since he's been here. He loved it so much he took the boys sledding and wore them out. (Fakhir wasn't scheduled to work yesterday. Though that didn't stop him from calling his boss and offering to walk a mile through the snow to cover for any-one who couldn't make their shift. The boss said the place was empty so no need to come in. I hope he was duly impressed with Fakhir's ded-ication. I sure was.)

When they came home from sledding we had grilled cheese sand-wiches and tomato soup for dinner. Are you remembering to eat and get enough sleep since the mortar attack? I'm sure things are even more intense than usual right now. But you'll be no good to anyone (yourself included) if you're not running on all cylinders. Promise me you're taking care of the basics like food and sleep.

The snow plows cleared most of the streets last night. Which means it was back to work and school today.

p.s. I almost forgot to tell you. When I went out to get the paper before work this morning, I found a card and a single red rose on the mat by the front door. The envelope was addressed to me but the card wasn't signed — it just had a big red heart on the front with a printed inscription inside — "Thinking of you on Valentine's Day." Do you know who sent it? Did you ask someone to leave it there as a surprise for me?

Thursday, February 14, 2008   11:56 p.m.

Happy Valentine's Day. Did you get my card? It's okay you didn't have time to send me one. We don't need a stinkin' holiday to say I love you. (I love you, by the way.)

Finn and Rory made a fuss over me after school. (Did you put them up to it?) They each gave me a homemade card with a lovely message inside. Rory gave me the cutest little stuffed monkey he bought at the school store and Finn made a mixtape of my favorite female singers. They even offered to take me out to dinner tonight but I reminded them I had already made plans to babysit Chloe for Wade and Isabel's night out.

I had a delightful time watching Chloe. She's four months old now and at that stage where she's putting everything in her mouth. The boys helped me put away a bunch of stuff before she came over, yet she still managed to find a dog biscuit between the couch cushions — which she promptly put in her mouth. (We won't share that last bit of information with Isabel, who would have a cow if she knew.) Other than eating dog biscuits, Chloe spent most of the evening looking at (and also trying to eat) Finn and Rory's old copy of *Pat the Bunny*.

Unfortunately Wade and Isabel's date didn't go so well. I could sense a bit of tension between them when they dropped off Chloe, but I figured the night out would do them good and things would be fine by the time they came back to pick her up. That turned out to be a big fat negatory.

I wasn't expecting them until nine o'clock at the earliest but the doorbell rang around eight and it was Isabel — by herself. She looked upset so I invited her to come sit down in the family room where I had Chloe on a blanket on the floor. It seems Wade drank too many margaritas at dinner, and his drinking was the very thing Isabel had been planning to talk to him about. And I guess the evening went downhill from there.

As you know, Wade's been struggling with alcohol since he came back from that last tour in Iraq. Then he got into that fight at the O'Club last summer and you had to refer him to the SACO. (His drinking had likely been a problem even before that last deployment, but up 'til then it hadn't affected his military career.) Once he got on the SACO's radar he seemed to be getting things under control. But then, when he retired from the Marine Corps in November, things started going off the rails again.

Three months have gone by since he got out and he still hasn't been able to find a job. I don't understand it — people say they want to help our veterans but why aren't they hiring these men and women? Wade's a retired major with an honorable discharge and 22 years of leadership experience.

But then he goes and gets a DUI on New Year's Eve. It's a miracle the charges were dismissed on a technicality — things could have turned out much worse. I'm not defending him in the least — he could have killed someone that night, including himself. He's just lucky he was out of the Marine Corps by that time. Had he gotten a DUI when he was still in, we both know it would have ended his career right then and there.

Isabel told me Wade's been trying to get an appointment at the VA so he can talk to a counselor about his drinking and some other issues. But the waiting list at the VA is like, three months long. Ridiculous! He needs help and he needs it now.

According to what Isabel told me tonight, the tension at home had been building well before he retired. She admits she'd been pressuring him to start looking for a job in the months leading up to his retirement. He kept saying he had too much on his plate what with wrapping things up at the unit, staying sober and convincing the SACO he had his shit together. She says things got even more stressful when Chloe was born in October. Of course they're completely in love with Chloe and they both dote on her, but we all know how challenging life with a newborn can be. Add in Wade's difficulties adjusting to civilian life plus him not being able to find a job — all of that compounded by his drinking — and the atmosphere at their house is rather strained of late.

She still has her job as a receptionist at the law firm, but even with Isabel's wages and Wade's retirement pay, they're bringing in barely enough to make their mortgage payments — let alone pay the rest of their bills. (I'm not sure but I get the feeling they over-borrowed when they bought that house — which might explain why they don't just sell the damn thing and rent an apartment or move closer to her parents. With housing prices falling the way they have in the last year, it's entirely possible Wade and Isabel are underwater on their mortgage.)

Fortunately their neighbor is an elderly retired woman who's been helping take care of Chloe for little or no pay when Isabel is at work. Now that Wade's not working he keeps Chloe with him most of the time, but the neighbor still helps out when Wade has places to go. (Isabel says that when Wade first retired he spent all day applying for jobs, but as time went on he began to get discouraged. Recently she discovered he's been dropping off Chloe at the neighbor's house after lunch, then making his way to the American Legion post where he ends up hanging out all afternoon drinking instead of sending out resumes.)

Isabel's parents and sister live in New Orleans (where she's from and where she met Wade when he was stationed at MCSF before coming here). And Wade's family is in Minnesota. So it's not like they have family nearby to help. (Welcome to life in the military.)

And that trip she went on a few weeks ago, when Wade was here for dinner and she and Chloe were in NOLA? She said the purpose of that visit was to get advice from her parents, who think the solution is for her to leave Wade and move back home with Chloe. But they've only been married five years. Isabel ultimately decided to come back and try to work things out. She was really hoping she and Wade could have a heart-to-heart tonight.

She must have been pretty upset because she's never confided in me like this before. Until now she's always been kind of standoffish whenever we see them at the Birthday Ball or other functions. (Not that I'm judging. I'm sure people say the same thing about me.) Nonetheless I told her we're here for her and Wade, and whatever they need, just ask. That's when she let me know she'd been so disgusted with Wade tonight she left him stranded at the restaurant without a ride home.

Holy crap! Here I had assumed she dropped him off at home before coming to our house to pick up Chloe. We'd been sitting there talking for at least 45 minutes!

When she told me that, I jumped up from the couch and said, "Well let's load Chloe in the car so you can hayaku out of here and go get Wade." She gave me a sheepish look, hemmed and hawed, then screwed up the courage to ask if I wouldn't mind going to get Wade myself. She was also hoping I'd bring him back here instead of dropping him at home with her and the baby. I guess the reason she was spilling her guts to me like that was the lead-in to her saying she needed a break from Wade. I wasn't sure bringing Wade back here was the best idea, but knowing she must be at the end of her rope, I agreed to go get him.

As luck would have it, Fakhir was just getting home from work as Isabel was leaving with Chloe. He offered to go with me to pick up Wade.

So he and I drive to the Mexican restaurant, where we find Wade outside in the freezing cold, passed out on a bench, wearing a sombrero. The waiters who were closing things down said he'd been sitting at the bar doing shots of tequila since his wife left. They wanted to call him a cab but he couldn't remember his address. I don't know why they didn't just look at his driver's license. Maybe they asked and Wade refused to give it to them, incoherent as he was. They were just getting ready to call the cops when we pulled up.

Fakhir and I managed to rouse Wade enough that he could drape an arm around each of our shoulders and let us help him into the back seat of my car. (Thank God Fakhir was with me.) Once we arrived back home, we repeated the process, guiding Wade into the house before laying him on the couch in the family room. Fakhir took off Wade's shoes while I covered him with a blanket. Wade, meanwhile, continued to mumble incoherently which caused Soda and Brig to get even more riled up than usual.

The boys, inevitably, came out of their rooms, wondering what all the fuss was about. I briefly informed Finn and Rory that Maj. Miller would be sleeping on our couch tonight. I didn't offer an explanation, nor did they need one. From the sombrero on the coffee table to Wade passed out on the couch, it wouldn't take a rocket scientist to figure out what was going on.

I wrote Wade a note saying I had to get up for work in the morning, but there'd be coffee in the coffee pot and he should feel free to hang out until I get home at four. I propped the note on the sombrero, where he'd be sure to see it when he woke up.

Things sure have gotten interesting around here since you left. Will you be able to call home this weekend? I miss the sound of your voice.

Friday, February 15, 2008   5:38 p.m.

Thanks for the photo from your stop in Kuwait a couple weeks ago. I showed it to the boys, and it made us happy to see your smiling face. It's too bad so many areas around Camp Victory are restricted from taking photos. Can you at least send us a picture of your CHU?

Are things settling down somewhat since the incident last weekend? Or is everyone still on high alert?

I loved reading your description of the change-of-command ceremony in the palace rotunda. I remember the general you mentioned from his rather long-winded speech at the Birthday Ball when we were stationed at Quantico. That was the time one of the Marines standing at attention for almost an hour eventually fell face-first into the cake, right? I also remember another Ball where a Marine passed out into a potted plant during the guest of honor's speech. (I assume that whenever you're invited to speak at these events you have enough sense to shut your pie-hole before people start passing out.)

I'll make sure the boys are up Sunday morning before your call comes through. It's been a while since you've talked to them. Sunday will work better than trying to call them after school when they're tired and generally uncommunicative. Rory has a hockey game tomorrow night so he can tell you all about it when you guys talk.

Work today was exhausting. At first no one was scheduled to be in ISS so I spent the morning catching up on incident reports. Around 10 a.m. one of the assistant principals brings a student named Marcus to my room. He'd been harassing some fellow students in gym class and refused to cooperate when the P.E. teacher instructed him to sit out. He ended up getting sent to the principal's office and she decided the best thing would be for him to cool his heels in ISS (effectively separating him from the students he'd been badgering).

He seemed friendly enough at first but I soon realized he was going to be vexatious. He asked if he could use the student computer to do his homework and I said of course. While I was working on my computer I kept an eye on what was on his screen and it looked as if he was on the school website. But after a while I noticed he was acting strangely — snickering and smiling and muttering. I casually got up from my desk and walked across the room to sharpen a pencil. From there I could see a small window in the bottom corner of his screen where he was obviously Skyping with someone. (Skype being one of many programs not allowed on school computers.)

I quietly approached Marcus from behind and asked him what he was working on. He quickly closed the Skype window and pointed to the school website. I told him let me have a look. I put my hand on the mouse and clicked to see what applications he was running. Sure enough he had a Skype session going. I quit out of the program, deleted it, and asked him how it got on the computer. He said it was already there. I said no it wasn't, because I checked the computer first thing this morning like I always do. He insisted he didn't know anything about it and that he wasn't Skyping with anyone (even though I saw it plain as day). I told him he had just lost his computer privileges and to go back and sit in his study carrel.

A little while later he had his hands in his book bag (which was laying on his desk) and I realized he was typing on his laptop — from inside his book bag! (You would not believe the skills these kids develop in order to stay connected to their technology.) So I had him put the bag on the floor next to his chair. The only things I allowed him to keep on his desk were a pencil and paper and a textbook. That seemed to work — at least until after lunch.

I was escorting Marcus from the cafeteria to the ISS room when he decided it would be fun to try and ditch me. He quickly ducked into the boys' locker room — knowing I wouldn't chase after him in there — and exited from the opposite side into a different hallway. By the time I got to the other side, he was nowhere to be found. I don't know what the little jerk thought I was going to do — say "oh well" and let him wander the halls the rest of the day? Hell no. Nor was I going to make an ass of myself playing hide-and-seek with a junior in high school.

I decided to go straight to the authorities. I press the Talk button on my walkie-talkie. "Officer Dempsey, this is the ISS supervisor. We have a student on the lam. Can you meet me in the south hallway outside the boys' locker room?"

Our School Resource Officer knows all the best hiding places. Without even knowing who he was looking for (we can't say students' names over the radio), he shows up five minutes later with Marcus in tow. Marcus is smiling widely, obviously proud of himself. I give him barely a glance.

"Thank you Officer Dempsey. Where'd you find him?"

"On the other side of the gym. Behind the trophy case," he says.

"Oh that's genius. Not like a hundred other kids haven't already thought of that one."

"Yep. Pretty obvious." Officer Dempsey turns to Marcus. "Try that again son and next time your mom will be called." He nods curtly and walks away, his radio already squawking again.

Marcus falls into step with me as I head back to the ISS room. "You wouldn't really call my mom," he says.

"Uh, yeah. I would. Actually — I would call the assistant principal, and she would call your mom." I could see he'd been enjoying testing me all day, trying to figure out how far he could push and what he could get away with. (I don't know how the teachers manage to get any actual teaching done when they have one student like this in class, let alone two or three.) I am so done messing around with Marcus, and I let my facial expression show it. They don't call it Resting Bitch Face for nothing.

Wisely, he remains silent.

I sense an opportunity for leverage. As I'm unlocking the ISS room door, I say, "Let's see how the rest of the afternoon goes. If you're cooperative, I won't write you up or call Mrs. Nelson. If not ... well, let's just say I'm done with your shenanigans Marcus."

The rest of the afternoon passed without incident. When the last bell finally rang, I was more than happy to get the hell out of Dodge.

By the time I came home Wade had showered, borrowed some clean clothes from Fakhir's closet, and straightened up the kitchen. He even had the dishwasher running. He offered to take the dogs for a walk while I write you this email. (Oddly enough, the dogs don't seem to have a problem with Wade. Maybe because they can tell he gives zero fucks whether they like him or not. With Fakhir it's a different story. I wouldn't call it outright warfare. More like a state of hostility between the two powers: Fakhir vs. The Dogs. Lots of empty threats on the dogs' side — well, except for Soda's tendency to latch onto Fakhir's pant leg — and a whole lot of propaganda coming from Fakhir's side — i.e. pretending the dogs don't bother him.)

As soon as Fakhir gets home from work we're all going out for pizza. Thank God for three-day weekends! (And yes, this time I remembered we're off on Monday.)

Saturday, February 16, 2008   7:27 a.m.

Sounds like the situation inside Camp Victory is getting back to normal (whatever that is). Have things changed much from the last time you were there? Your job is different this time, right? That's probably why you're still trying to get a feel for things. Bet you'll be glad when you're not the FNG anymore.

Isabel left a voicemail on the home phone last night while we were at dinner. Turns out she doesn't want Wade to come home for another few days. I told him he could camp out here until she decides to take him back. I mean, what else is he going to do? I hope you're okay with that. You and I have known Wade since our first tour on Okinawa all those years ago, when he was still married to his first wife. I always liked

Shelley. But I don't blame her for wanting out. Wade was a player, even then. Fifteen years of that and she finally had enough. Guess it was a good thing they never had kids.

Wade looks up to you, Liam. When we were out for pizza last night he couldn't stop talking to the boys about what a great boss you've been and how much he respects you. (Fakhir chimed in several times to agree.) It made me happy to hear them say such nice things about you in front of Finn and Rory.

Fakhir and Wade are hilarious together. I knew they'd worked on the same missions in Iraq, but I was under the impression it had been a while since they'd last seen each other. If that's true, last night they picked up right where they left off. The two of them had us laughing so hard people in the restaurant were looking at us. They remind me a little of Finn and Rory. If there's anything I've learned after having two sons, it's that guys give each other non-stop shit only because they love each other.

After we got home from dinner Finn scrambled around looking for a costume to wear to an "ABC" party. (As Finn explained it, "ABC" means you're allowed to wear Anything But Clothes.) He ended up making an outfit for himself out of aluminum foil (with a little engineering assistance from Fakhir). The entire process was quite entertaining (including a lot of eye-rolling on Rory's part). In spite of the no-clothes rule, I insisted Finn wear boxer briefs underneath the foil in the event of a wardrobe malfunction.

When Neil, Crystal, and Darryl pulled up, we had them come inside so we could see what they were wearing. Neil had covered himself in yellow crime scene tape while Darryl somehow managed to piece together an outfit using playing cards and duct tape. Crystal's ensemble featured blue-tinted plastic wrap — you would have enjoyed seeing that. (Wade certainly did. Oh, and so did Rory. He was staring so hard at Crystal's strategically wrapped chest I thought he might injure himself.)

After they left, Josh came over to play video games with Rory. I know we normally don't let the boys have friends over when they're grounded but Rory's been on his best behavior since the Jack in the Box incident. Besides, he caught me in a good mood when we were on our way home from the pizza place. (Now, if he had asked to have Ethan over, that would've been an entirely different story.)

Fakhir called it an early night since he had to work the breakfast shift in the morning (having mastered the biscuit vs. bagel vs. muffin situation). I asked Rory and Josh to keep it quiet down in the basement so they wouldn't disturb Fakhir. But Fakhir told us not to worry, he can fall asleep anywhere, anytime, under any circumstances. (Gee, that sounds familiar. Must be a military thing.)

I'm sure we get on Fakhir's nerves sometimes but he is unflappable. Well, nearly unflappable. The pets continue to find ways to irritate him, hard as he tries to pretend they don't. The cats, for example, have begun leaving hairballs right outside his door at night. Soda, for his part, continues grabbing onto Fakhir's pant leg every chance he gets. Brig has let up a tiny bit on the barking—except if Fakhir tries to sit in your chair in the family room. Then she goes apeshit. Fakhir has given up on even trying to sit in that chair, except sometimes he forgets. At which point Brig resumes her guard-dog duties and barks ferociously at Fakhir until he un-asses himself and finds another place to sit. It's become something of a joke around here. (Though sometimes I wonder if Fakhir sits in that chair on purpose, just to get a rise out of Brig. A proxy war of sorts?)

So that left Wade and me to entertain ourselves the rest of the evening. Truth be told, I would've liked nothing more than to go upstairs, put my jammies on, and curl up in bed with a good book. But I could see Wade needed companionship so I put on a pot of coffee and suggested we play a game of Scrabble at the kitchen table.

I confess: I assumed I'd beat Wade by a landslide. But it turns out he's an excellent Scrabble player in his own right. He kicked my ass on a triple word score with "qadi." Who the fuck knows what a qadi is? Apparently Wade does—he tells me it's a Muslim judge. I argue it's an un-Anglicized foreign word and therefore not allowable. He counters it's a commonly used word by U.S. military forces in the Middle East. I think that's a stretch, but I decide not to challenge him since he's beating me anyway. Were you aware of Wade's secret identity as a Scrabble nerd?

Playing Scrabble seemed to relax Wade, and over the course of a couple games, he opened up to me about what's been going on between him and Isabel. He admitted his drinking has become a problem again. I couldn't help but smile and say, "Well duh. Hello sombrero sitting on our coffee table." He laughed and said, "Yeah I know. That's all on me." He also said he knows he can't do it alone and that he's working on getting help. He's determined to stay sober this time.

But it so happens there's a lot more to their money problems than Isabel let on when she was giving me an earful the other night. During Wade's last two deployments since they've been married, Isabel has gone overboard on spending, according to Wade. He says she was supposed to be putting his combat pay into a special savings account, but instead of doing what they agreed upon, she spent all the money on a new living room set before he even got back to the States. She also racked up some department store credit cards, and last year she used their tax refund to buy Chesty. (That's the English Bulldog she got from a breeder as a "surprise" for Wade last summer.)

Wade said he and Isabel have started seeing a financial counselor, but with him not having a job, the bills are piling up. (And he confirmed my suspicion that they're underwater on their mortgage, which is why they don't put the house up for sale and move into something more affordable or closer to Isabel's parents.)

Add a four-month-old baby into the mix, and things are beyond stressful for the two of them. And who knows what else might be going on? Wade rarely talks about his combat experiences (unless it's to tell a funny story), but you have to wonder if multiple deployments have finally begun to leave their mark on him. At any rate, I don't think it's a coincidence his drinking has increased with each tour overseas these last five years.

I asked Wade about his family, if they could help with any of this, and he says his parents are elderly and he doesn't want to worry them. Evidently Wade is the youngest of six children—he was a "surprise" baby long after his folks thought they were done having kids. His next-oldest sibling, a sister, is severely disabled and lives with his parents. So I can understand why Wade is worried about being a burden on his family—but for fuck's sake, he could really use some support right now. I asked about his other siblings, all of whom live in Minnesota not far from the parents. Wade says, "It's complicated." Something about him not being close with his older siblings due to the age difference and their resentment over him not coming home enough to help with the parents and disabled sister. (Like, what do they think? Wade can just pick up and take two weeks' leave in the middle of a deployment to a combat zone because his jackhole siblings think he should spend more time in fucking Minnesota? What the hell?!)

If only Wade could get in to see someone at the VA sooner than three months. He's clearly in a crisis situation. Why can't they bump him up on the waiting list, ahead of others whose situations aren't as urgent? Or is everyone on the list in crisis?

Tell me what else we can do for him, Liam.

5:08 p.m.

I braved the commissary today even though it's Saturday and yesterday was payday. But I had to go. We've been going through groceries faster than usual lately what with the extra people in the house.

Have I mentioned we've been giving Fakhir cooking lessons? When he first got here, it quickly became obvious he'd never prepared a meal for himself in the 27 years he's been walking this earth. When I asked him about it, he said his mom and sisters always cooked for him at home, and when he got involved with the military he ate MREs and chow hall food.

Then he told me that when he was living with the Salazars, Janet cooked three square meals a day, every day of the week. (Bless her heart. Not gonna happen in this house. When you're deployed, I consider it a major accomplishment if I pop a frozen lasagna in the oven and open a bag of pre-made salad for dinner.)

Once I became aware of Fakhir's lack of cooking experience, I could see why he'd come to our house with the expectation his meals would be prepared for him. By me.

And, I'm sure it wouldn't surprise you in the least to learn that I quickly disabused him of that notion.

Our first order of business was teaching him to use the microwave to reheat leftovers. He's starting to get the hang of that. A few days later Rory taught him to make toast. (Seriously — the guy didn't know how to work a toaster. In fact he still doesn't — I've never seen someone burn so much toast in my life. It's a good thing they don't have him on the grill at McDonald's! I mean, how does a guy who can disassemble and reassemble his M-16 in under a minute not know how to work a toaster?)

Despite Fakhir's problems with toast, Finn was somehow able to teach him to heat up frozen pizza and Taquitos in the oven. Last week I taught him to boil water for pasta. Next on the agenda: scrambled eggs. We might be getting ahead of ourselves on that one.

When I first suggested the cooking lessons to Fakhir, you could tell he wasn't too keen on the idea. But once he heard "The Colonel" (as he refers to you) not only cooks — but also bakes — he quickly got on board. It further helped our cause when Fakhir observed Finn making stir-fry for dinner one night and Rory making macaroni and cheese another night. Soon we'll have Fakhir working the program too.

Better sign off for now. Tonight is Rory's hockey game, and all of us are going.

It was only a month ago you left, but it feels like a year.

Sunday, February 17, 2008   7:03 p.m.

I'm happy Finn and Rory had the chance to talk with you this morning and tell you about what they've been doing lately. Strange though how you had to hang up so quickly — did someone important walk up to your desk, or something unexpected come up?

Everyone was in a great mood after Rory's game last night. Fakhir is now an expert on slashing, spearing, high-sticking, and cross-checking. Do you think it was bad that he and I had a couple beers during the game in front of Wade? Wade told us he didn't mind, and that he'd gladly be our DD. But I wonder if we shouldn't have drank at all in front of him. I don't want to make things harder for him than they already are. I'm going to remember that next time. Wade hasn't had a drop of alcohol in the three days he's been with us. He already looks healthier. His color is good and the twinkle in his green eyes is coming back.

He wanted to go running today but there's still a lot of icy patches outside so I suggested he come with me to my drop-in yoga class this afternoon. He pooh-poohed the idea but I dragged him along anyway. As we drove to the strip mall where the yoga center is, he made the whole thing out to be a big joke — and he was pretty giggly the first few minutes of class. But after a while I could see he was really into it. (Or really into the instructor, who — as I'm sure you recall — is stunning in her natural, glow-y way.) Regardless, Wade said he felt invigorated by the time we came home to start dinner, and he wants to go back. I said he could keep my extra mat and I also loaned him one of my yoga DVDs to take home.

Isabel still hasn't returned any of his calls and I've decided that if she doesn't call him back by tomorrow, I'm going to call her myself. It's high time she lets him come home, especially since he's been sober.

I'm thinking of calling Col. Phillips at home tomorrow (he should be off since it's President's Day). I want to see if he knows someone at the VA who can help Wade get in to talk to a counselor sooner than three months. Unless you have any better ideas? Wade could also look for an AA meeting out in town, but he seems more comfortable around other veterans — people who can relate to multiple deployments and the challenges of transitioning to civilian life.

No school tomorrow, no plans for tonight, and I couldn't be more delighted. Finn is at work, and Rory's in the basement with Fakhir and Wade playing Mario Kart. (I can hear them yelling at each other all the way from up here in our bedroom.) I told them I was retiring early for the night. Came upstairs with a bowl of popcorn, put my jammies on, and am now settled in bed with the pets and the new David Sedaris book, *When You Are Engulfed in Flames*. (Seeing as you're not here to make me laugh, he's the next best thing.)

A bunch of cars are parked in front of Agnes' house. I thought at first she was having that fundraiser for Congressman Roper but then I remembered that was last week. Tonight she's having one of those trunk parties where you invite a bunch of women over to drink wine and try on clothes until everyone's drunk enough to buy a load of shit they'll never end up actually wearing. She called earlier and asked if I wanted to come — all the women in the neighborhood are there — but I told her it's been hectic, and tonight I need a night to myself. (Besides, no way am I trying on clothes in front of twenty women, no matter how much wine is involved.) Agnes made her typical attempts to twist my arm but I cut her off. (My bullshit meter has been pegged as of late.) Surprisingly she gave up more easily than usual, and told me if I changed my mind to just come over. I think I'll be happier snuggled up here in our bedroom. Ever since you went away, I feel lonelier in a crowd than I do when I'm alone.

Monday, February 18, 2008   10:52 a.m.

Happy President's Day. I don't suppose you guys get a day off? (And what would you do with it anyway?)

Thanks for the note and the heads-up regarding a possible trip to Fallujah in the coming weeks. I understand the need to be ambiguous about your travel plans, but at least now I won't worry if I haven't heard from you. (Still, if you're away from the base and you get anywhere near a computer, please drop me a quick email just to let me know you're safe. And if you don't have access to a computer, well, I'll try my best not to have any more freak-outs.)

Sounds like you've had a lot of rain and it's pretty muddy there. What a mess. Does it get much below 40 degrees at night in Baghdad during the winter? You didn't say anything about why you had to hang up the phone so quickly yesterday. I'll just assume it's Top Secret and if you told me you'd have to kill me.

I was able to get through to Ken Phillips this morning. He said he doesn't know anyone personally at the VA but that he'll call the appointment line himself to see if he can get any further up the chain than Wade did. I don't know how Ken pushing buttons on an automated phone system would be any different than Wade doing the same thing, but maybe Ken will get through to a human being who has some authority to prioritize Wade's case. It's worth a shot.

I also spoke to Ken's wife Tammy, who answered the phone when I called. She said Ken was taking the kids to the new Shrek movie later today and invited me to meet her for lunch. While I'm not usually one for spur-of-the-moment get-togethers, I surprised myself by saying yes. So I'm meeting her at one o'clock at the iHOP you and I like to go to sometimes. I haven't been there in months — I'm looking forward to some double blueberry pancakes with whipped cream. (It'll be nice to catch up with Tammy too.)

Meanwhile Isabel still hadn't returned any of Wade's calls so I talked it over with him this morning and he said it was okay for me to go ahead and call her myself — thinking she'd finally pick up the phone if she saw it was our number instead of Wade's cell. When she did pick up — as expected — I dispensed with the pleasantries and got straight to the point: It's time for Wade to come home. She hesitated, but agreed to come pick him up this afternoon.

Wade is encouraged by the way things are going at the moment and I have to say I'm feeling hopeful too. That was a great idea you had to look for a veterans-in-recovery program out in town. I didn't know such things existed but it makes a lot of sense. When I told Wade about your idea over coffee this morning, he got on the computer right away to start searching for a group in the area. With all of us working together, maybe we can help Wade get the help he needs. He sure seems ready to get back on track. I only hope Isabel is ready too.

p.s. Soda has taken a liking to Wade, and I think Fakhir is jealous. Early this morning when Fakhir came upstairs from the basement to leave for work, Soda was curled up on Wade's chest while Wade slept on the family room couch. I'd been sitting quietly at the kitchen table, drinking my coffee and reading the paper. Fakhir didn't notice me there, obviously, because I overheard him talking to Wade and I don't think either of them would have said what they said if they'd known I could hear them. But I heard — and saw — everything.

Fakhir walks over to the couch to get his shoes (which he'd left on the floor nearby). As soon as he comes close, Soda bares his teeth and starts growling at Fakhir. Fakhir leans over to pick up his shoes, and as he does so he says to Soda in a low, threatening voice, "You better watch your back you little turd."

Wade's eyes are still closed but he cracks a smile and says, "I heard that. I'm gonna tell Emilie you've been talking smack to her Chihuahua. Maybe then she won't think you're so goddamn perfect."

Fakhir, slipping into his shoes, replies, "Are you blackmailing me asshole? You want me to tell Emilie the only reason you're going to yoga with her again is 'cuz you wanna bang the teacher?"

Wade, eyes open now (but still smiling), says, "Yeah well fuck you, twatwaffle."

"Yeah and fuck you too douchenugget. I gotta leave for work now so I'll let you alone to cuddle with your little Chihuahua. Maybe you can teach him to lick your balls for you."

With that Fakhir heads toward the door — but he has to walk through the kitchen first.

He passes by me sitting at the kitchen table, and I make sure to keep my head down, as if engrossed in the paper. "Good morning Fakhir," I say without looking up.

"Good morning Emilie," he replies, without missing a beat.

As he exits the kitchen I catch a glimpse of him holding his head high, staring straight ahead with a perfectly neutral expression, as if nothing had happened.

I listen as the door clicks shut. I glance back at Wade, who's pretending to be asleep, the trace of a smile still on his lips.

Tuesday, February 19, 2008   7:48 p.m.

Isabel finally came to get Wade yesterday after I got home from my lunch date. She still seemed aggravated, and they didn't talk much as the boys and I said our goodbyes to Wade. I told Wade I'd call to check in with him in a few days, and reminded him that Fakhir and Col. Phillips said they'd keep in close touch also.

My lunch with Tammy was great. I'd forgotten how refreshing it can be to chat with another military spouse. She filled me in on all the latest gouge from the unit — stuff I normally don't care much about but didn't mind hearing today. It got me thinking again how I sometimes miss living on base (just the tiniest bit). Living off-base does have its advantages and disadvantages. Disadvantages are: We're not surrounded by military people all the time. Advantages are: We're not surrounded by military people all the time. Seriously though. We've met a lot of great people at our various duty stations. And many of them have become lifelong friends. We've been lucky that way, when it comes to military neighbors. (And on the rare occasion we did live near an asshole family, we only had to put up with them until the next set of PCS orders.)

We sent you a birthday package. I hope you don't have to be in Fallujah on your birthday, although from what I hear it's a party town.

Wednesday, February 20, 2008   5:09 p.m.

So you got to ride in the Rhino Runner. The boys are jealous. (And, I have to admit, I'm kinda jealous too.) Rory wants one for his birthday. And if you can't bring home a Rhino Runner, he says he'll take a Humvee. Seeing as he'll be getting his learner's permit soon, an armored vehicle would probably be a good idea.

I had three boys in ISS today. I showed them a picture of the Rhino Runner which I found on Wikipedia. They thought it was pretty awesome. They were fairly well-behaved. I had a nice conversation with one of the boys who's an avid reader. If you don't mind, I'm going to lend him your copy of Into the Wild. He likes outdoor adventure stories and hasn't read that one yet. The other boy was a bit of a jokester. (He'd been assigned to ISS after making a pie crust in the shape of a penis in Culinary Arts class.) The third boy was quiet — kind of a sourpuss actually.

I managed to get a smile out of him, however, when I did my quarter trick at the end of the day. One of the boys had asked me about it as soon as he came in this morning—said he heard I can catch a stack of 22 coins off my elbow but he didn't believe it. I told the three of them if they worked hard on their homework all day I'd do the coin trick for them before the last bell. And, if they were really good, I'd give them a chance to try beating my record. (I think the world record is something like 50 quarters, but I believe I hold the school record at 22. Not too shabby.)

Like I said, the one boy (Derek) was kind of a grouch—didn't talk to anyone during lunch (just scowled at everybody), and stayed hunched in his study carrel the rest of the time. But at the end of the day when I said they'd earned a personal performance of my quarter trick due to their good behavior, he perked up right away. The three boys watched intently as I carefully placed the coins on my elbow, and when I caught all of them in my hand with one swift movement, Derek got such a big smile on his face it practically melted my heart. By the time the bell rang all three of them were standing in the middle of the room trying to catch quarters off their elbows, laughing and smiling and talking.

All in all, a good day.

Thursday, February 21, 2003   9:22 p.m.

After I wrote yesterday's email to you I made an impromptu decision to go to Bunco with Wanda last night. Yes—I, Emilie Mahoney, went to Bunco. Wanda had sent me an email earlier in the day saying I was welcome to come along with her if I felt up to it. She's been very understanding about my need for alone time during your deployment, and I know she wouldn't have minded if I said no thanks. But I'm starting to feel like kind of a jerk for saying no to people all the time. So I guess maybe she caught me at a weak moment. Or my desire for people to not think I'm a jerk finally outweighed my desire to be alone. Turns out

I should know better than to say yes to stupid shit like Bunco just so people will like me. Or maybe, I really am a jerk.

Wanda gave me a lift to the home of the woman who was hosting. I'd never met her before, but I did notice her name in the email that Wanda had forwarded to me.

She opens the door and invites us to step inside. Wanting to start the night off on a friendly note, I extend my hand and say, "Thanks for having me over, Chancee." (Rhymes with Nancy. Or so I think.) But instead of returning my handshake, she offers me three of her fingers. I awkwardly hold onto her fingers, moving my hand up and down as if it's a real handshake. (What else was I supposed to do? Curtsy?) And then, instead of saying hello or something like that, she says, "It's ShaunSAY."

I look at Wanda like, "Is this person for real?" but she refuses to catch my eye. (The least she could have done was warn me in the car on the way over how to pronounce ShaunSAY's name — instead of waiting until I get schooled by ShaunSAY herself.)

So we make our way down to the basement and it turns out I don't know any of the people there except for Wanda and maybe one other person (and my new BFF ShaunSAY). In spite of a rocky beginning, I make a quick recovery, and as we begin the first few rounds, things seem to be going okay. You already know how much I dislike Bunco but I'm giving it the ol' college try, rolling the dice and drinking the wine and being sociable all at the same time. And I'm doing a pretty damn good job of it too — until we switch tables and I end up sitting next to a woman named Pamela.

She looks familiar and it takes me a minute but then I remember: She was the one at Back-to-School Night last fall with the fake tan and six-pack abs, walking around in boy shorts and a workout bra, her blonde hair in a big ponytail on top of her head, acting like she was the one in high school instead of her daughter — remember her? At least this time she's a little more covered up — as in, a tennis skirt and halter top. In the middle of winter. (She is wearing a pair of Uggs however — a look no doubt borrowed from her teenage daughter.)

After we're introduced, Pamela says, "You're the one whose husband is in Afghanistan, right?"

"Well, Iraq. But yes, he's ... away right now."

"Please tell him from us we said thank you for his service," she says, giving me the dreaded puppy-dog eyes. Then, looking around the table to all three of us, she continues, "I think we should just bomb the heck out of those Iraqis. Can you even believe we're still letting Muslims into the country?"

With this my heart immediately begins pounding against my chest. In fact it's thumping so hard I wonder if everyone else can hear it. Wanda and the other woman at our table are listening in silence, their own mouths apparently not working at the moment. Before Pamela can say anything further, I open my mouth to speak, having no idea what's about to come out. "As a matter of fact, Pamela — that is your name, right? — we have an Iraqi national living in our house at the moment. He's like family to us." I stop myself from saying anything else in an effort to not escalate the situation. (In hindsight I should have just gotten up and left right then and there.)

"Oh. I didn't realize that," she replies, seemingly unfazed by my revelation. She takes a swig of her Kiwi Sauvignon. "Whose turn is it to roll?" she asks.

"I think it's mine." Wanda quickly picks up the dice in front of her and we resume playing.

The other woman at the table (whose name I forget) starts talking about the Turnabout Dance at the high school last month and the rumor going around that the principal wouldn't allow a certain student into the dance because she was falling down drunk. I know who the student is, because I'm the one who typed up the incident report. But that's confidential information so I remain silent. I do, however, arrange my face into a pleasant expression as I listen to the chatter and take my turn with the dice. I'm hoping Malibu Barbie feels chastened enough to keep her ignorant thoughts to herself. Or at the very least, maybe we'll switch tables before she starts going off again.

Unfortunately my hope is misplaced. A few more rolls of the dice (and swigs of wine) later, Barbie/Pamela starts yammering about a woman at Whole Foods who wears a "burqa."

"Have you seen her pushing her cart around the store?" Barbie asks. "She can barely see where she's going with that burqa thing on her head. The other day she turned a corner and practically ran me over!"

"Are you sure it's a burqa she was wearing?" I ask. "Maybe you mean hijab?" My heart is starting to pound again.

"Hijab, burqa, whatever," she says, waving her hand dismissively at me. "You can call it anything you want." Barbie turns her attention to the other women at the table. "She still looks like a ninja."

Wanda doesn't laugh (thankfully) but the other woman (let's call her Xenophobe #2) covers her mouth and lets out a titter.

At this point I've had enough. I carefully set down my wine glass and plaster my most innocent smile on my face. "You know, Barbie—uh I mean Pamela—I think the women who cover themselves in head-scarves and beautiful fabrics look way more alluring than the women who traipse around town half naked wearing workout gear. Don't you?"

Before she can respond I get up, pressing my fingers to my forehead. "Oh dear. I feel a migraine coming on. Wanda would you mind taking me home a little early?"

"No—not at all." She stands up quickly, eager to put an end to what will surely be remembered as The Bunco Night From Hell.

Wanda and I stop briefly at ShaunSAY's table to offer our apologies before making a hasty exit up the basement stairs. As we reach the landing I can't help but turn back for one final goodbye. "Goodnight Chancee!" (Rhymes with Nancy.)

Outside, I breathe in the cold night air. My pounding heart starts to slow again.

Wanda and I sit for a moment in her car, engine running, seatbelts fastened, the both of us staring straight ahead. She exhales loudly, causing her lips to puff out. "Well *that* was awkward."

I want to ask Wanda why she didn't speak up when Pamela was say-ing those terrible things. But I'm either too tired or too chickenshit or both. It's one thing when you realize someone you barely know is preju-diced; it's another thing entirely to start that conversation with a friend. Instead I say, "I suppose you won't be inviting me to Bunco again."

"Who knows if they'll even invite *me* back," she replies good-naturedly. Wanda puts the car in drive and pulls away from the curb. "I'm the one who brought you."

Friday, February 22, 2008   8:43 p.m.

Finn and friends are in the garage practicing some new songs. They've finally come up with a name for the band — The Smoking Lamps. How do you like it? Finn (being the only military brat in the group) is the one who came up with it. I think it's rather clever, even if it is a Navy term. At the moment they're learning to cover T. Rex's "Mambo Sun," which I can hear all the way up in the bedroom. At least they have decent taste in music.

Fakhir went over to Wade's tonight. Isabel is visiting her parents in New Orleans again (this time without Chloe). Fakhir offered to keep Wade company and help out with the baby. I'm not sure how things are going between Wade and Isabel, but the trip to see her parents — so soon after the last one — is worrisome. On the bright side, Wade did find a veterans-in-recovery program out in town that he's attended twice already. (Ken hasn't had any luck with the VA, so Wade's next appointment is still three months off.)

I had Marcus again in ISS today. Remember him? He was the one who was in last week, Skyping and running off and generally wreaking havoc. Today was more of the same. I tried engaging him in conversation as a way of forging some sort of connection with him (or, at the very least, distracting him from his troublesome ways). But he makes up the wildest stories. For instance, he told me his family is extremely wealthy (they live in a mansion, have nine cars, etc.). Yet I know he and his mom live in the apartment complex down the road because of the ISS notices we mail home.

He seems intelligent but at the same time, he clearly does not give one shit about school. Or about being nice to people. I suggested he write a letter of apology to the student he'd been picking on yesterday (the reason he was put in ISS today), but he refused to even consider the idea. A few of my kids write some really nice apology letters when they're in here, but not Marcus. I wonder if he even knows what it feels like to be sorry.

I've never had a student quite like him. Usually after spending a few hours or an entire day together, I'm able to establish at least a passing connection with each student. But when I talk to Marcus, it's as if there's no one there behind the wire-rimmed glasses. To be honest, he kind of creeps me out.

I have my jammies on, ready to watch "Bridge on the River Kwai" on TCM in a few minutes. Remember when we watched it with your parents when you and I were dating? Your dad made popcorn in the fireplace while we snuggled under the orange-and-green afghan your mom crocheted. I never appreciated watching old movies — until I met you.

Did you know the song the British soldiers whistle in Bridge on the River Kwai has lyrics? It didn't originally have words — they were added later, at the beginning of World War II, by the British. And do you know why the soldiers in the movie whistle the song instead of singing the words? It's because they're too raunchy! Here's an earworm for you:

Hitler has only got one ball,
Göring has two but very small,
Himmler has something sim'lar,
But poor old Goebbels has no balls at all.

Let's watch this together when you come home. (And speaking of balls, tell yours hello from me.)

Saturday February 23, 2008   11:22 p.m.

Happy Birthday. I haven't heard from you in a few days so I'm guessing you finally made that trip to Fallujah. I hope you at least got our package before you left.

Rory's final hockey game of the season went well — they won 5-3. Rory took a couple slapshots from the point, one of which went in. The kids were in great spirits at the team pizza party afterward. I know you would've enjoyed it. We missed you.

I'm afraid I have some bad news to share (though it's possible you already know). Someone has been threatening Fakhir's mother and sisters back in Baghdad. Fakhir spoke to his mom on the phone this morning. She says they started receiving threatening phone calls a few weeks ago — whoever is calling says stuff like "traitors" or "spies" and then hangs up. She also said the phone calls are becoming more frequent.

Fakhir was clearly disturbed when he got off the phone. He told me he asked his mother why she didn't tell him about all this as soon as it started happening. It seems she kept thinking it would stop and she didn't want to worry Fakhir unnecessarily. But since the calls have increased, she felt she had no choice but to finally let him know.

As I'm sure you're well aware, this isn't the first time the family has been threatened. Fakhir told me some other things you may or may not already know. It started when the insurgents discovered Fakhir was helping the coalition forces — about halfway into his three years working with the Marines. Various security precautions were put in place (Fakhir didn't elaborate), and for the most part he and his mother believed the threats would subside once he left Iraq and came to the U.S. Things did quiet down the first couple months he was here but now it seems his family is being targeted again, all because of Fakhir's work as an interpreter.

I wonder if the insurgents think Fakhir is still in Iraq? Or are they targeting his family to make an example of him? To send a message to anyone else who might be thinking of helping the Sunni Alliance or U.S. and Iraqi forces?

After he got off the phone with his mom and briefly filled me in, Fakhir called Major Salazar in Twentynine Palms. (Ray and Janet and the kids are settling in — well, as much as any family can "settle in" to temporary lodging.) Fakhir asked Ray if he could find out what's taking so long with his mother's and sisters' visas. Ray promised he'd be all over it with the State Department come Monday morning, but we really don't know how much he can do, if anything. In previous phone calls to the State Dept., the only thing they tell Ray is that Fakhir's mother's and sisters' visas are "in progress" — nothing more. I'm sure Fakhir's own visa was expedited since he was employed by the U.S. military and already had the proper clearances. But the background check on his mom shouldn't be that difficult. I mean, come on — she's a 63-year old woman!

His sisters say they're planning to go to Norway to live with one of the uncles. Maybe going that route will help get their visas processed more quickly. It's situations like this that make our shitty little problems seem like, well, shitty little problems. We owe it to Fakhir to keep his family safe.

Speaking of staying safe, I hope your travels to and from Fallujah are without incident.

I love you.

Sunday, February 24, 2008   4:26 p.m.

Fakhir found out last night that Ahmad's family is being targeted as well. They've received the same threatening phone calls, and Ahmad's younger siblings have stopped going to school out of fear for their safety. There are stories of other interpreters in Iraq who've been kidnapped, tortured, shot. No doubt the Americans in Baghdad are well aware of these incidents. Is there anything you can do, or anything you know that you can share with us?

It's getting to Fakhir. Since he spoke with his mom yesterday, he's stopped joking around with the boys like he usually does, and spends more time in his room. I can't say I blame him. I don't know how he's holding it together even this much. Last night I explained to Finn and Rory what's going on so they don't think Fakhir is upset with them or anything. They feel terrible for him, and so do I.

Fakhir says without his job at McDonald's to keep his mind occupied, he'd go crazy with worry.

Monday, February 25, 2008   8:11 p.m.

Still no word from you. I read in the paper that the Pentagon said about 8,000 of the troops that were sent to Iraq as part of last year's surge won't go home this summer as planned. The article quoted a three-star general who said that even though there's been a sharp drop in sectarian violence (along with a drop in U.S. casualties), support troops like MPs and helicopter crews and HQ staff are still needed to "preserve that progress." That's all well and good but what about our service members who've been there a year or more and thought they were going home this summer? What about their families? How much longer will they be expected to hang on?

I didn't tell the boys you're probably in Fallujah. I'll tell them where you were after I know you're safely back inside Camp Victory. No sense adding to their concerns.

We are all gloomy around here. To make matters worse, I cracked a molar the other night. But don't worry—I have an appointment with Dr. Hermey after work tomorrow, and I'm sure he'll fix me up in a jiff. Still, I wish you were here to make us laugh again.

Tuesday, February 26, 2008   9:01 p.m.

I had my dentist appointment with Dr. Hermey today. He said I've been grinding my teeth in my sleep again and that's why my molar cracked. He put a temporary crown on it and he also fitted me with this crazy-looking headgear thing I'm supposed to wear to bed every night. Which means you can stop worrying about me finding a boyfriend while you're gone. Unless I find someone with a mouth appliance fetish.

When I got home from my appointment I found a notice from the city on our front door. It's a citation for not bringing in our trash cans by 7:00 last night. You have got to be fucking kidding me. (And by the way, don't go getting mad at Finn and Rory. They're good about pulling in the empty cans when they get home from school. And if they forget, Fakhir or I will do it. But I'm sure you can understand we've all been somewhat distracted lately. Worrying about our trash cans is not a top priority at the moment.)

I called the city to see if it was because one of the neighbors complained. The lady who answered the phone wouldn't say. I find it hard to believe any of our neighbors would rat us out for letting our empty cans sit on the curb one extra night — especially since they all know you're in Iraq. Or do you think Agnes might have done it because she's still secretly pissed about the whole Jack in the Box thing?

Whoever did it, I hope they go straight to hell — without a drop of porter to quench their thirst.

Wednesday, February 27, 2008   10:44 p.m.

Book club tonight was great. I hadn't realized how much I needed to be among friends until I got there. Genie made a shrimp scampi dip I couldn't stop eating. (She gave me some to "take home for the boys," but I hid it in the bottom drawer of the fridge, underneath a bag of organic spinach.)

Patty, as per usual, kept checking her phone and texting from the moment she arrived, even while Genie was trying to give her presentation about the author. So every time Patty's phone goes off with a text alert (the same annoying chime Jack Bauer's phone makes on "24" when he's getting a call from the CTU), Genie gets all discombobulated and loses her place in her presentation. Even I wanted to smack Patty upside the head about the third or fourth time her stupid ringtone went off.

Finally the next time Patty's phone goes off, Barb, who'd had a few too many wine spritzers during cocktail hour, says to her, "Unless you're actually getting texts from Kiefer Sutherland, could you please put your damn phone on silent so the rest of us can listen to Genie's presentation in peace?"

God I love these women! And in spite of that little kerfuffle we ended up having an excellent discussion about the book. (This months' selection was *Einstein's Dreams* by Alan Lightman. So much to love about this book — I'm sending you my copy.)

And as usual, some pretty entertaining conversations followed our book discussion, including a spirited debate over whether "Atonement" or "No Country for Old Men" should have won the Oscar for Best Picture. In fact the debate became so lively at one point it seemed Agnes and Patty might come to blows after Agnes made a throwaway comment about Kiera Knightley having only one facial expression. I thought Patty was going to cry when she heard that but what do you expect from someone whose favorite movie is "The English Patient"? As for me, I thought "Lars and the Real Girl" should have won Best Picture. (And I certainly wouldn't kick Ryan Gosling out of bed for eating crackers.)

Speaking of eating crackers in bed, I miss you and am wondering how much longer you'll be in Fallujah. As nice as it was to get out tonight, I've been feeling uneasy after a week of not hearing from you. I'm trying my best to stay calm but it's getting harder each day.

Stay safe, wherever you are.

Thursday, February 28, 2008   12:42 p.m.

Just a quick note from work while I'm on my lunch break. Our security system went haywire last night. The first time the alarm went off, around midnight, it scared the hell out of me. After I shut the stupid thing off, I went around the house carrying your machete from Colombia, checking all the doors and windows, the dogs following behind me. Soda still hasn't figured out he's a Chihuahua, so he was ready to take down any intruders. Brig, on the other hand, seemed to think we were up for a late-night snack. I assumed Fakhir had fallen asleep with his headphones on, because he didn't come upstairs to see what was going on. The boys did come out of their rooms but I told them to go back to bed, everything's fine, probably just a short in the alarm's electrical system. Either that or a serial killer hiding in the linen closet.

But then the damn alarm kept going off the entire night, every two hours. I'd jump out of bed, punch in the code, and go back to sleep until the next time it went off. I felt like that guy on "Lost" who had to get up to push the button every 108 minutes in order to avert some sort of worldwide catastrophe. Only I didn't have Sayid there to fix the computer for me. Damn. That would have been nice. Nonetheless, do you think I was being tested by the DHARMA Initiative?

6:53 p.m.

Update: By the time I got home from work Fakhir had fixed the alarm system. That was a huge relief, because I was exhausted after having been up most of the night.

In fact I'm feeling kind of asshole-ish right now because I snapped at Finn and Rory a few times after they got home from school. I was getting dinner ready and it seemed like every time I turned around one of them was at my heels. I had to keep saying "Make a hole, make a hole," so as not to bump into somebody with a hot dish or a saucepan. (We were having SOS in honor of you. It would have tasted better if Fakhir hadn't burned the toast again.)

And then during dinner Finn and Rory got into an argument over which of them takes the longest showers. By that time I had zero patience left and I told them—not in a very nice way—to shut their pie-holes, they were both wasting my oxygen along with the planet's water supply.

I know. That was shitty of me. After that, Fakhir and the boys cleared the dishes in silence and I came up to the bedroom to write you this email. We're all a little on edge lately. I'm worried about you, and about Fakhir, and Fakhir's family. Fakhir has more reason than any of us to be worried. But he's not acting like a jerk. I'm sure Finn and Rory can feel the tension, and they're worried and anxious too. I should have been more patient with them. I'm going downstairs right now to apologize to everyone.

Friday, February 29, 2008   4:44 p.m.

It figures you'd be deployed in February during a leap year. That's one more day and one more night added on to an already unbearably long year of living life without you.

I've been thinking about those families whose service members were part of the surge and are now being told they won't get to come home this summer. That won't happen to you, will it? Would they extend your deployment beyond the original twelve months? I know it's foolish to think anything is set in stone with the military. (There's a reason they say there's nothing permanent about Permanent Change of Station orders.) But I'm trying to convince myself they won't need you to stay on any longer than a year. All the news outlets are saying the situation in Iraq is getting more stable. Right?

No news on the visas. Ray Salazar did talk to someone at the State Department but he keeps getting nothing more specific than the visas are "moving along" or "in progress." Fakhir has been talking to his mom almost every day now. The threatening phone calls haven't stopped, but at least they haven't escalated beyond verbal threats.

The calls are being made to the family's landline, which is both good and bad. Good in that they don't have Fakhir's mom's mobile number (we think), but bad because if they're calling the landline the insurgents probably know where they live. My thought would be to just rip out the damn landline but Fakhir says they don't want to do that for fear it might push the insurgents to do something more aggressive. I asked him why can't they trace where the phone calls are coming from? Fakhir explained that al Qaeda uses prepaid disposable phones, and they destroy each phone after one use. So then I wondered why can't they just figure out where the terrorists bought the phones like they do on NCIS? He says it doesn't work that way in real life, especially not in Iraq.

Fakhir is understandably tense. The boys and I are doing our best to support him. We're all hanging in there, taking things day by day. (Even so, it sure would be nice to hear from you.)

I spoke to Wade during my lunch break today. After Isabel came back from NOLA and learned Wade had started attending a veterans-only AA program, she agreed to go for marriage counseling with him. I offered to watch Chloe while they go to their appointment next week. Luckily Wade had the wherewithal to enroll in Tricare for Retirees after he got out, so he's covered until he switches over to the VA.

They're allowed a certain number of self-referred family therapy sessions with a provider out in town, which means he and Isabel can get started right away.

Wade did have a bit of news on the job front. He got an offer to work overseas as a civilian contractor in Qatar. A Marine Wade knows is over there now and referred Wade — it's not like Wade applied for the job or sent in a resume. But Wade told me he'd only work in Qatar as a last resort if he and Isabel absolutely needed the money. He knows his best chance of working things out with her would be to stick close to home. And I'm sure he doesn't want to do anything that would put his sobriety at risk. Going overseas again — even as a civilian — could be bad for his recovery.

I'm taking Finn and Rory to see Coraline tonight. I think a movie will provide some much-needed mother-son relaxation time, and maybe it will make up somewhat for my shitty behavior of late. They'll still be able to get together with their friends afterward since we're going to an early show. (Making them spend an entire Friday night with their mother would be just plain mean.) I'm even going to let them have whatever they want to eat at the theatre, and that's going to be our dinner. (Here's hoping no one sees us making a meal of Slurpees and Junior Mints, lest they call the authorities.)

This talking into a vacuum is getting old. You'd better get back to the base soon, before I start freaking out and call the HMFIC demanding to know where the hell you are.

Saturday, March 1, 2008   3:19 p.m.

I treated myself to Starbucks while out running errands this morning. (I would have stopped at Fidelia's but I was all the way on the other side of town and Finn wasn't working anyway.) When the barista rang up my order she asked if I wanted to buy a pound of coffee "to donate to the troops." I couldn't help but smile. I was tempted to say, "How about if we skip the middle man and you just hand over that pound of coffee to me? I'll take it to the post office and mail it to my husband straightaway? Or

better yet, how about free lattes for a year for all us military spouses?"
But I kept my mouth shut — for once. In fact I gave her an extra twenty
to cover the cost of one of those pounds of coffee for the troops, and
told her to keep the change.

p.s. I think something is screwed up with your paychecks. I thought
your IDP was supposed to kick in once you arrived in Iraq, but the
amount being deposited is the same as always. Would you be able to
look into this once you get back from Fallujah? Or should I call Ken
Phillips at the unit to see if anyone there can look into it? And why does
this happen every time you go on deployment? One would think they'd
have this figured out by now.

Sunday March 2, 2008   6:53 p.m.

I came across a BBC news item online that said a leader of one of the
Sunni Awakening Councils was killed in a suicide bombing in Fallujah.
Could that be one of the people you were meeting with there? The
article said the Sheikh and his aide were killed along with all five
members of al Qaeda in Iraq who carried out the attack. I know you're
well-protected wherever you go but. ...

You know what? I need to stop reading the paper and watching the
news and surfing online news sites. Total news blackout.

(How long do you think *that's* going to last?)

I decided to take a nap instead of going to yoga this afternoon.
(Wade went without me.) While I was asleep, the boys did some of their
chores. And when I woke up, Fakhir had come home from work and
the three of them were in the kitchen making fish sticks, frozen peas,
canned corn, and toast. (And Fakhir only burned some of the toast this
time.) I'm not complaining — it was a lovely dinner.

We miss you.

Monday, March 3, 2008   5:08 p.m.

Finally! You're safe. What a way to start the day, knowing you're back inside the base. Will you be able to send any photos from your trip to Fallujah? Or how about a photo of the V-22 Osprey you took there and back? The boys would love to see that.

I understand you haven't had time to gather intel on what's going on with Fakhir's family yet. You've been back less than a day and you still have to get snapped in with your regular job. But if and when you do hear something, will you let us know right away?

Glad you liked the package we sent, but sorry you missed opening it on your birthday. We figured the M&Ms in the trail mix wouldn't melt this time of year, and the extra chapsticks are for you to share with anyone who needs them. The framed pictures of us are to add to the collection in your office.

I put a rump roast in the slow cooker before I left for work this morning, so we're having Italian beef sandwiches for dinner. I'll sleep much better tonight knowing you're back to spending nights in your CHU.

Tuesday, March 4, 2008   8:36 p.m.

After a good night's sleep I woke up this morning with more energy. I hope you were able to get a good night's sleep too. I meant to ask — where do you sleep when you're on missions like the one you just went on?

I had Lucia in ISS today. Remember her? She was the one I had back in January, with the animal print thong who wants to go to cosmetology school. She's been missing a lot of classes lately so she got written up and sent to me for the day.

She walked in all grumpy again just like the first time she came here, throwing her book bag in the study carrel and barely saying a word. Instead of ignoring her unfriendly behavior like I did last time, I called her out on it.

"Oh, come on Lucia. You're not gonna give me a hard time again are you? I thought we were on good terms by now. And besides, I wore my purple eyeliner today."

That catches her interest and she can't resist taking a closer look at my eye makeup. When she sits down, I pull a chair up to her study carrel and we chat for a few minutes about cosmetics. Once she relaxes a bit, I get around to talking about what I wanted to talk about all along.

"So what's going on with all these unexcused absences lately?"

She looks down and shrugs her shoulders. "I don't know. Just tired I guess."

I take a look at the incident report in my hand. "It looks like you've been mainly missing your first hour class, Language Arts. Is there a problem with the teacher or someone in the class?"

"No. I like Mrs. Callahan a lot," she says. "And I get along fine with everybody in there."

"Help me understand why you keep missing that particular class then," I say.

She keeps staring down at her lap. "Like I said. Just tired."

"You mean you're oversleeping?" If that's the case she probably has a bunch of tardies too, which haven't been noted on the write-up.

She nods her head without saying anything, still not meeting my eye.

"Do you have a hard time getting out of bed in the morning? I happen to know a certain 17-year-old boy who has the exact same problem."

At that she cracks a smile and looks up at me. "You mean Finn Mahoney? He's your son, right? Me and him have a class together. Nutrition. 7th hour with Mr. Zim."

"Yep, that's him. One and the same." Now that I've gotten her to smile I want to get back to the matter at hand. Turning serious again, I ask, "Is there anything going on at home that's making it harder than usual to get up in the morning? You weren't missing your first hour class last semester."

She goes back to looking at her hands, which are in her lap, and starts picking at her blue nail polish. While giving her time to answer I have a chance to inspect her makeup, which looks smudged — like she put it on the day before and then slept in it — and her hair doesn't look much better. Usually when I see her in the hallways between class periods her makeup and hair are flawless.

She stops picking at her nail polish, raises her head and starts talking. "I'm usually pretty good at waking up. But my aunt and uncle have been living in our apartment with us and they have a newborn baby who's colicky. I love my cousin and everything but she keeps me awake most of the night."

"Can't you close your bedroom door?" I ask.

She shakes her head. "My aunt and uncle are staying in my room with the baby. My three brothers share a room together, and my parents have their own room. I'm on the pull-out sofa in the living room. So when the baby's up all night I hear everything."

I run the numbers in my head. Eight people plus a newborn in a three-bedroom apartment. All I can think to say is, "That must be really hard."

It's enough to open the floodgates. Lucia begins talking in earnest. "My dad got laid off from the Ford assembly plant. He's been there 20 years and they just cut him loose — him and a bunch of other people — for no reason."

I remember reading in the paper not long ago the plant had laid off hundreds of workers.

She continues, "I mean, money's always been tight, but now it's even tighter. I make decent money from my tips at the hair salon — I'm just a shampoo girl now but I want to be a stylist."

"I remember," I remind her.

"I help my parents out with groceries and stuff. And my aunt and uncle pay what they can too. My mom stays home with my little brothers — child care is too expensive, we couldn't even afford it when my dad was working. But now ... I don't know if my parents are going to be able to pay the rent. I heard them talking about it one night in the kitchen when they thought I was asleep."

"I'm sorry," I say.

"I'm behind on my homework because I work after school and I can't get any homework done at night because after I come home from work and eat dinner I'm so tired I end up falling asleep. And then I wake up a few hours later when the baby starts crying. I finally fall back asleep around four and that's when I oversleep and miss first hour."

"First and foremost we've got to figure out a way for you to get some sleep, Lucia. Is this something you can talk to your parents about? Maybe if you all put your heads together you can figure out a better sleeping arrangement?"

"Yeah, I can talk to my parents about pretty much anything."

"Okay. That's the first item on your To Do list. Next thing is we have to figure out a way for you to show up for class and get your homework done. If you keep missing Language Arts you could fail that class. And if you don't get that credit you're not going to be allowed to graduate. That would be a shame, since graduation is only three months away ..."

My thoughts wander to Finn. I can hardly believe he's going to be done with high school in just three months.

Lucia says something but my mind is far away. "I'm sorry, what did you say?" I ask.

"I said I don't care if I graduate or not. I don't need my diploma to be a stylist anyway."

"Mmm, I'm pretty sure you do need your diploma, Lucia," I say, my attention now fully back on her.

"My boyfriend Brian says I can be a stylist without it. He didn't finish high school — he dropped out last fall — and he says he's doing fine."

"Is that so?" I say quietly. I want to ask more about Brian, like what it is exactly he's doing so fine at, but I decide to keep the focus on her. "I'm almost positive if you want to go to cosmetology school you have to have either your diploma or a GED."

She looks at me, still skeptical.

"How about if we go online and look it up?" I suggest.

We get up out of our chairs and walk over to the student computer. I let Lucia have a seat while I stand next to her. She opens up a new search window, her fingers poised uncertainly above the keyboard.

"Just google state regulations for cosmetology school or cosmetology licensing requirements or something like that," I say.

She ends up on a page with the state licensing requirements, and sure enough, it says right there you need to have either a high school diploma or a GED before you can even take the licensing exam.

"Okay then," I say. "Second thing on your To Do list after getting enough sleep is to finish high school. Add a bullet point under that one, making a note to pass Language Arts."

She actually gets up and walks back to her study carrel, pulls a spiral out of her book bag, sits down again and begins making a list. "What's number three then?" she asks.

"That's something you'll need to decide for yourself. While you're thinking about that, how about if we split my peanut butter and jelly sandwich? All this talking has made me hungry."

Lucia spent the rest of the day getting caught up on her assignments, and before the final bell rang we spent a few more minutes on the computer looking at some cosmetology schools in the area. I still don't know how she's going to be able to get a good night's sleep what with the newborn baby in the apartment, or what's going to happen to her family if they can't pay their rent, but Lucia did promise me she'd try her hardest not to miss any more classes. I asked her to stop in and see me one day next week just to let me know how things are going.

Finn had his piano lesson after school and afterward the boys and I went to O'Shannons for our weekly dinner out. All three of us ordered bangers and mash, but they weren't as good as the ones you make.

What have you been eating in the chow hall? Have you had any opportunities to try some native Iraqi dishes when you're traveling? Fakhir says he really misses his mother's upside down chicken. I told him he should get her recipe and maybe he could try making it. He said no way he'd be able to cook one of his mother's dishes, and besides, he's just now figured out how to boil water and reheat leftovers. (Still working on the toast thing.) Maybe he's right about the upside down chicken.

Wednesday, March 5, 2008   9:02 p.m.

I'm sorry to be the bearer of more bad news. One of Fakhir's sisters found a note on their front gate saying something like, "Collaborators for the Americans. Leave." So now we know for sure the insurgents know where they live. Fakhir's mother and sisters have stopped going out, but they can't stay locked up inside forever. His youngest sister Farah is the same age as Finn. She's trying to finish high school but now Fakhir's mom won't let her leave the house to go to school. Some of the neighbors have started helping, providing food and bringing Farah her homework assignments, but they're taking a big risk. If the insurgents see the neighbors helping the al-Azzawis, it's all but guaranteed they'll be targeted too.

As soon as Fakhir got off the phone with his mom tonight he said he was going to call Ray Salazar to see if Ray can get in touch with someone at Camp Slayer.

"Why don't you just email Liam to see if he can contact someone at Camp Slayer?" I ask. "I mean, he's right there in Baghdad."

"Emilie, the colonel is already burning the midnight oil at both ends," Fakhir replies.

I want to explain he really means burning the *candle* at both ends (or just burning the midnight oil) but I figure now is not the time. I make a mental note to mention it to Fakhir later, when he's not under so much stress.

Instead I say, "But I still don't understand why you're asking Ray to get in touch with someone at Camp Slayer, since he's out in Twentynine Palms and not that much closer to Baghdad than we are."

"Ray and I were both assigned to Camp Slayer at one point," Fakhir explains. "We worked together on one of the intel teams. We know a couple of guys there who can help us. They're our best hope."

"I see. Well then. Carry on."

Fakhir calls Ray, who says he'll get on it first thing in the morning when he can call from a DSN line. Then Fakhir calls Ahmad, who reports nothing further has happened to his family since the last time they spoke. Thank God.

As Fakhir hangs up from Ahmad, a look of sheer exhaustion crosses his face.

"Fakhir, I'm sure your manager at McDonald's would understand if you called and asked for a few days off."

"Why would I want to do that? My job is what's keeping me going right now. When I go to work tomorrow, I'm asking my manager for more hours, not less."

Liam, I understand your plate is more than full. I also understand you can't venture out in town without putting a lot of other people's lives at risk (not to mention your own). So checking on Fakhir's and Ahmad's families yourself isn't an option. I did tell Fakhir I'm keeping you apprised of the situation, and that I asked you to find out what you could on your end. He got a little mad at me for even mentioning any of this to you. But I knew you'd be upset with me if you found out about all this from someone else (which you undoubtedly will), and then on top of that, found out that I knew about it but didn't say anything to you. So there you have it. Damned if I do and damned if I don't.

Thursday, March 6, 2008   10:11 p.m.

Tonight Fakhir helped me watch Chloe while Wade and Isabel went for their marriage counseling session. Chloe absolutely adores Fakhir — every time she sees him she holds out her arms to be held — even if I'm already holding her. (A much warmer reception than he gets from the dogs, I might add.) He seemed to take comfort in Chloe's hugs and slobbery kisses.

Ray Salazar called earlier to let Fakhir know he got ahold of one of their former team members at Camp Slayer (who's on his fourth deployment to Iraq). Turns out they were already aware of the increasing threats to Fakhir's and Ahmad's families, and they're working on "a plan." Did you have anything to do with that? If you do know anything, I gather you can't tell me about it in an email. (Probably not in a phone call either, right?)

I have no idea what type of safety precautions they're putting in place (and if Fakhir knows he's not saying) but I could see the tension leave Fakhir's jaw and shoulders as soon as he spoke to Ray. We realize it's going to take a while to implement any sort of plan to keep their families safe, but it's an immense relief to know someone over there has eyes and ears on the situation. With Ray also working the State Dept. angle, we're hopeful for some good news one way or another.

Things must have gone well with Wade and Isabel. After their appointment, Wade called and asked if we wouldn't mind watching Chloe a little longer while they stopped to grab a bite to eat. I said of course, they should plan on doing that every Thursday. I'm sure they have a lot to talk about.

Fakhir fed Chloe some mashed bananas and baby cereal, then I gave her a bath and put her pajamas on. Even Finn and Rory took a break from doing homework to come play with her for a while. Since she's starting to crawl now Brig and Soda are a little unsure what to make of her. They can't figure out if she's an animal or a person or what. But they do like licking her fingers in search of errant baby food.

Remember when Finn and Rory were that age? You were always so good with them. And even though you were gone a lot when they were little, they were never shy with you when you came back. This will be the longest you've ever been away from them. I'm glad at least they're older now, and can understand why it is you're gone. They're very proud of you, you know. I hear them talking about you to their friends, telling them what you're doing and what things are like for you there.

I've heard other military wives say they feel distant and disconnected from their spouses when they're deployed, but for me it's the opposite. Being apart from you reminds me of all the things I love and miss about you, like what a good father you are to Finn and Rory and how you try to make up for your long absences by being extra kind and thoughtful to me when you're home. We're thousands of miles away from each other, yet I couldn't feel closer to you.

Friday, March 7, 2008   8:29 p.m.

Fakhir talked to his mother before he left for work this morning. Although he couldn't be specific, he was somehow able to reassure her that people are working behind the scenes to help keep the family safe.

When he's talking to his mom on the phone, Fakhir speaks mostly Arabic, but sometimes he slips into English — maybe because he's used to speaking it all the time here. We happened to both be in the kitchen getting a cup of coffee when I couldn't help but overhear something he said in English. They were finishing up their conversation and it sounded like he said, "I know Mama, I wish Baba was here too." I really wasn't trying to eavesdrop — we were both standing in front of the coffeemaker at the time. I pretended I didn't hear anything and went about my business.

But it got me to thinking. Baba means dad in Arabic, right? I know Fakhir's dad died some years ago, but that's pretty much all I know. Do you know what happened to him — what he died of or how he died? Fakhir doesn't say anything about it other than his dad passed away when Fakhir was in college.

Meanwhile Fakhir's job at McDonald's is going well. He likes his coworkers, and his manager says he's doing great. (The manager also gladly gave Fakhir more hours when asked.)

An added bonus is that Fakhir comes home with the funniest stories sometimes. At the dinner table tonight he told us a story about a construction worker who came in during the lunch shift and asked for a free cup of water with his quarter pounder and fries.

"People in Iraq, they can hardly believe it when I tell them restaurants here give out free water," he explains. "With ice. And free refills."

"How come?" Rory asks.

"Well, a lot of people in Iraq don't have clean water. Some people walk long distances every day to get their water from the Tigris or Euphrates. But even that water is contaminated."

"Why is it contaminated?" Rory asks. (I'm pretty sure that kid is going to grow up to be a scientist of some sort. His curiosity is endless.)

Fakhir patiently continues. "A lot of reasons. The water level is dropping because of drought, dams being built upriver, infrastructure not being maintained, and damage from the war. Almost half of Iraq is desert, so a lot of people depend on the rivers for water."

Even Finn is interested now. He finishes chewing his bite of pizza and asks, "Why doesn't the military just bring these people some water?"

"They do. They've been giving water to people since the war started. And they're trying to help rebuild the infrastructure. The Red Cross and other aid workers bring water to people too. But lately even the military has stopped going into certain areas. The insurgents are targeting anyone — it doesn't matter if they're military or civilian — who tries to deliver water to people."

"What a bunch of shitbirds," Finn says, shaking his head. He's concerned, but not enough to stop him from grabbing another piece of pizza.

"All right," I jump in, wanting to lighten the mood. "This is all quite fascinating. But I'm dying to know what happened with the construction guy at work today."

Fakhir wipes his mouth with a napkin, gives me an understanding nod, and continues. "Okay. So this guy asks for a free cup of water. I give him his tray of food plus an empty cup for him to fill with water at the drink station — just like we're supposed to do. The lunch rush is almost over and there's no one at my register, so I get a chance to watch this guy at the drink station. And you know what he does? Instead of filling his cup with water, he fills it with Hi-C Orange! The bastard! He stands there, gulping down the Hi-C Orange, plain as day. It's like he doesn't even care if anybody sees him. And then, to add salt to injury —"

"Wait!" Rory interrupts. "Did you just say 'add salt to injury'?"

"Yes."

Rory and Finn look at each other, then at me.

"You're the one who brought it up," I say to Rory. "Go ahead and explain." I take a huge bite of my pizza and sit back in my chair to watch the show.

"What are you guys talking about?" Fakhir asks.

Rory explains. "Dude. It's supposed to be 'add *insult* to injury'. Not 'add *salt* to injury'."

Fakhir appears to weigh the two options in his mind. "I think 'salt' makes more sense," he says. "I mean, if you're injured, and you add salt to the wound, isn't that a lot worse than adding insult?"

"Well, yeah, that does make sense," Finn says. "But it's still two different sayings. It's either 'add insult to injury' or 'rub salt in the wound'. You're not supposed to combine them."

"It's called a mixed metaphor," I say, rejoining the conversation. "Like when you take two common phrases and put them together. A lot of people do it — even Americans."

"But Fakhir does it more than anybody," Rory adds.

Fakhir looks at Rory as if his feelings are hurt. "Thanks bro."

"How about if we get back to the story," I suggest.

"Okay. So to add *insult* to injury," Fakhir continues, "After the guy finishes drinking his first cup of Hi-C Orange, he puts his cup under the fountain and fills it again! With more Hi-C Orange! And I'm right there behind my register, watching him!

"I'm really pissed, you know, because this guy is drinking our Hi-C Orange without paying for it. But I know my manager wouldn't want me making a big scene over it. He's all about 'the customer is always right' and that kind of stuff. So what I do is, I grab a cleaning rag, and I come out from behind the counter and I walk real casual-like over to the drink station, and I start wiping it down. This guy is still standing there guzzling his contraband Hi-C. I'm pretending to concentrate real hard on cleaning but what I'm really doing is inching closer and closer to this assclown."

Finn and Rory have forgotten about the pizza on their plates, completely engrossed in Fakhir's story.

Fakhir continues, "So as soon as I get close enough for the guy to hear me — I don't look up or anything, I just keep wiping the area in front of the soda fountain — I say real quiet-like, 'I can't make you pay for those drinks you just stole but I can strongly encourage you to step away from the drink station'.

"I can see the guy out of the corner of my eye, just standing there smirking at me with his big-boy construction helmet and oversized tool belt. And I'm sure he's thinking something like, 'Who is this loser in a McDonald's uniform acting like he's a tough guy?' So at this point I look up from the invisible spot I'd been cleaning and stare intently into the guy's eyes, you know, like I'm Clint Eastwood in High Plains Drifter?"

"Oh man, my dad *loves* that movie!" Rory practically shouts.

"So what happened next?" Finn asks.

"I stare real scary-like into his eyes and I say, 'I can also tell you that I never, ever forget a face. And after you leave here today? It would be a good idea for you to never, ever come back'."

"Holy fuckballs!" Rory shouts.

"Rory! Watch your language," I say.

"You let Finn say shitbirds just a minute ago," he argues.

"That's not the same as fuckballs," I reply. "And besides, you're three years younger."

Rory rolls his eyes as if I'm the most annoying mother in the universe.

"Can we just get back to the story please?" Finn says.

Fakhir picks up where he left off. "At first he tries to be a hard-ass, like he's kind of laughing at me, but I can tell he's getting nervous, because he glances over his shoulder to his construction worker buddies sitting at a table nearby. They're watching us, and I can tell they're trying to figure out what's going on. Hi-C Orange Guy looks back at me and I'm still staring at him, and I'm thinking about that line where Clint says, 'You know you're going to look awfully silly with that knife sticking up your ass' — but I don't actually say that, I'm just thinking it. He's still standing there kind of frozen, like he can't make up his mind what to do. So what I do is, I go back to wiping down the drink station, and without looking at the guy, I say, 'You still here?'"

"And then what?" Rory asks.

"He takes his food tray and does this tough-guy walk to his buddies' table and sits down. I can hear them ask him something and he just shakes his head and says something under his breath, then the other guys laugh like they're all in on the same jagoff joke.

"I go back to my station behind the register and start taking orders again. But every chance I get, I stare across the restaurant at the guy while he's wolfing down his quarter pounder and fries. Last thing I do before he gets up and leaves is, I put two fingers to my eyes and mouth the words 'I'm watching you'."

Saturday, March 8, 2008   8:28 p.m.

Finn finally heard back from the music school in Chicago and they're giving him enough scholarship money to make it affordable — *plus* he's eligible for the work-study program so he'll be able to earn extra money during the semester. He's so excited! He has yet to hear back from the two other schools he was accepted to regarding scholarships, but since the one in Chicago is his top choice and they've offered him what he needs in the way of financial assistance, we're going to send in his deposit right away.

Finn's piano recital is three weeks away and he's close to having his piece memorized. He's been practicing late into the night. Rory and I are used to it but I wondered if Finn's playing was keeping Fakhir awake, and he said no, he loves falling asleep to the sound of Finn playing (when he's not listening to his iPod).

Rory has decided to join the track team now that hockey season is over, so he's been staying after school for track practice lately. I wish I had half his energy!

Tonight's agenda includes folding laundry and watching "Days of Wine and Roses" on TCM. Another one of my favorite movies with a bleak ending. I read somewhere that when he heard the studio was considering a lighter ending after filming had wrapped, Jack Lemmon flew to Paris so he'd be unavailable for any reshoots. And that both Jack Lemmon and Lee Remick sought help from AA at some point after the movie was made. (Which makes me wonder if Wade has ever seen this one?)

They are not long, the days of wine and roses:
Out of a misty dream
Our path emerges for a while, then closes
Within a dream. — Ernest Dowson

Sweet dreams to you, and goodnight.

Sunday, March 9, 2008   5:08 p.m.

We lost an hour this morning with Daylight Saving Time — does that mean we're only eight hours behind you now? I miss having you here to change all the clocks like you usually do. I'm tempted to leave them as they are. They'll be right again in seven months anyway.

9:22 p.m.

Dear family and friends:

Liam recently returned from a trip to Fallujah and is safely back inside the Green Zone. Since it's the rainy season everything is muddy. He says it won't be long before temperatures rise, so he asked me to relay the message not to include chocolate in any care packages after April 1st since it will melt. (But there's still time to send chocolate if you mail it right away — last care package I sent took about a week and a half.) The post office recently started offering discounts on flat-rate boxes being shipped to APO-FPO addresses in support of our troops overseas.

Other than that Liam seems to be getting along okay, though he misses everyone back home. He says his living quarters are more than adequate, but he's hoping to get moved to a CHU with running water when his name comes up on the waiting list. I'm enclosing a photo of him in front of the V-22 Osprey that took him to and from Fallujah.

Finn, Rory, and I are getting along okay too. Thanks for all your phone calls, cards, and emails. I'm sorry if I haven't answered each of you individually — most of my free time is spent writing emails to Liam. Our Iraqi houseguest, Fakhir, has been a big help to all of us since he moved in at the end of January. We'll be having a graduation party for Finn in May and hope all of you can come celebrate with us, where you'll also be able to meet Fakhir.

Until next time,

Emilie

Monday, March 10, 2008   10:09 p.m.

Arrrgh. You told me before you left you'd be inside the Green Zone, and I never heard otherwise from you since you got to Iraq. So I've been telling everyone your base is inside the Green Zone. Now you tell me Camp Victory and the Green Zone are two entirely separate areas of Baghdad? Whiskey Tango Foxtrot?! Where are you in relation to Camp Liberty and Camp Slayer, and what the heck is the difference between the International Zone and the Green Zone? I guess I'll just go online and look at a damn map.

You're welcome for sending out that email by the way. I put a lot of work into the emails I send to friends and family, not to mention all the emails I write to you. Now I feel like a total asshat for sending out wrong information.

Tuesday, March 11, 2008   4:18 p.m.

I'm sorry I was snarky in my message to you last night. I'm sure you were grateful but it just didn't come across in your email. I thought you'd be a little more appreciative. Plus, I was pissed off and embarrassed I've been giving wrong information to people. I try so hard to get things right, to understand what it must be like for you there, to do what's best for you and the boys and to try to keep up communications with everybody so people will still feel connected to you and won't forget about you while you're over there. I know they won't forget about you, but I want people to keep sending you cards and emails so you'll feel supported and loved. That's why I send out those emails to family and friends. So I guess it just hurt my feelings when all I got from you in response was nothing but a correction that felt like a criticism, even if that's not the way you meant it.

I know you must be under a lot of pressure and most days you only have a few moments to dash off a quick email with just a sentence or two. I know you don't have time to sit in front of the computer thinking up flowery lovey-dovey things to say to me. I'd much rather receive the one-sentence emails from you than nothing at all. So I'm sorry I lost my shit last night after I got your email. I felt horrible all night long and all day at work today. I was mad at you, and yet terrified something would happen to you before we had a chance to make up. I'm sorry for snapping at you. I love you and miss you. I'm not mad anymore.

Wednesday, March 12, 2008   11:47 p.m.

Remember Marcus, the troublesome kid I've had in ISS a few times? Apparently he joined the track team at the urging of the P.E. teacher, who thought it would be good for Marcus to do some more physical activity or something. So guess who ends up being on the high jump squad with Rory? Yep. Marcus. Even though Marcus is a junior and Rory's only a freshman. And the squad is a tightly-knit group of kids, so I guess Marcus and Rory have had quite a bit of contact since the season started a couple weeks ago.

Eventually Marcus put two and two together and figured out that the mean ol' In-School-Suspension supervisor (me) also happens to be Rory's mom. No one has ever given either of the boys any grief about it before—I maintain a pretty low profile at the school out of consideration for them. And it's not like Finn or Rory go around bragging that their mom is the ISS lady. So it's never been a problem for either of them.

Until now.

Come to find out that at the last few track practices Marcus has been making disparaging comments to Rory about me, like "Your mom is such a bitch," and "Aren't you embarrassed to have your Mommy working at the school?" and basically stupid shit like that. So far Rory just walks away when Marcus starts in on him, but it's getting to him.

By the way, I'm hearing all this from Finn—Rory hasn't said a word to me about it. I did notice Rory's been more quiet and a little on the grumpy side lately, but I just thought he was going through some normal teenage hormone fluctuations like Finn did at that age. Turns out that when Finn picked up Rory from track practice before dinner tonight, the two of them got to talking during the car ride back to the house and Rory confided in Finn about what's been going on.

Finn was concerned enough that when I was reading in bed tonight he came into our room to tell me about it. Rory swore Finn to secrecy, therefore Finn tried to make me swear I wouldn't tell anybody or say anything to Rory. I told Finn I couldn't promise that, but I'd at least sit on the information a few days until I (we) figure out the best course of action. I'm glad Finn told me and I don't want to break his trust with me or with Rory, yet I don't think I can just sit back and allow Rory to be bullied like that, especially because I feel responsible. If I didn't work at the school this wouldn't be happening to Rory.

I hesitate to even mention anything about it to you, because I don't want to add to your stress. But you always have such a common-sense approach to these things that I thought you might have some good ideas on how to handle it. My initial instinct is to hunt down Marcus at school first thing tomorrow morning and tell him to back the fuck off. Yet I know that would be the absolute worst thing I could do. Finn is upset too, and mentioned the idea of talking to Marcus himself. (I'm sure whatever Finn could think of to say to the little shit would be much more colorful than anything I could dream up.) But I convinced Finn not to do or say anything to anybody until I had a chance to email you and see if you had any brilliant ideas on how to approach the situation.

It's tricky, because I'm afraid if I report Marcus to the administration it might just make things worse for Rory. And then what are they going to do about it—put Marcus in ISS with me again? I could have a word with the track coach and ask him to keep an eye on the situation. Finn did ask Rory if the coach knows what Marcus is doing and Rory said he didn't think so, Marcus saves his taunting for when the coach isn't nearby. Sneaky little fuck.

I feel bad for Rory. Our family is under enough pressure already. To have this asshole giving our son shit just makes me want to cry.

Help?

Thursday, March 13, 2008   9:29 p.m.

It must be terribly frustrating for you to be halfway around the world when you'd like nothing more than to be here with us, offering your guidance and support. But you're being more helpful than you realize just by responding to my emails and sharing your thoughts and suggestions. I'm glad we're thinking along the same lines on this.

Finn told me that instead of coming home from school today and going back later to pick up Rory, he decided to stay after and hang around the field where the track team practices. (Which was especially nice of him, because temperatures here are in the 40s, the ground is still soggy from all the melted snow, and the wind has been whipping like crazy.) Finn made a point at the beginning of practice to go up and talk to Rory in front of Marcus, saying something like "Hey little bro" so Marcus would know they're brothers. Then Finn positioned himself inside the fence right next to where the high-jump squad does their jumps, and he stood there the entire time, until practice was over. Turns out Finn's tactic worked—his presence there was just enough of a warning for Marcus not to be an asshole to Rory.

My only concern is that Finn can't stay after school every single day of the week to watch Rory practice, since he has other things to do like go to work. Finn and I talked about the situation again tonight while Rory was in his room doing homework. I told Finn you think a good first step would be for me to talk to the coach. Finn's concern with that is Marcus might ratchet up his bullying once he finds out someone told the coach—like picking on Rory outside of track practice. And knowing Marcus, I agree that's a strong possibility. Rory seemed like he was in a little better mood at dinner tonight so I promised Finn I'd give it a couple more days before doing anything to intervene. Are you OK with that?

I babysat Chloe tonight while Wade and Isabel went to their counseling appointment. I invited them to have dinner with us beforehand but they seemed rushed and said they'd have to take a rain check. Wade did tell me he got a callback on one of the resumes he sent out a few weeks ago—it's for a position as a warehouse manager at a Mondo fulfillment center. It seems like a pretty good job, and Wade's

Marine Corps leadership experience makes him a perfect candidate. Only problem is, the fulfillment center is three hours away. And since they still have a lot of debts to pay off, even if Wade got the job, they'd still need the income from Isabel's job to make ends meet. So Wade would have to be a geo-bachelor during the week and come home on weekends. I know a lot of military families do the commuter thing, but considering Wade and Isabel's circumstances at the moment, this job doesn't sound ideal.

But I'm getting ahead of myself. We'll burn that bridge when we come to it, as Fakhir would say. This is just the initial callback from the person who specializes in veteran recruitment at Mondo. (Veteran recruitment? The more I hear about this company the more I like it.) Wade will have to make it through a series of phone interviews before he even gets an in-person interview, let alone a job offer. I'll keep you posted on how things develop. Wade is excited. Just getting a positive response after all the rejections he's had the past five months is a big boost to his confidence.

It seems like their marriage counseling sessions are helping. I haven't asked Wade directly about it but so far they both appear relaxed and happy when they come to pick up Chloe after their appointments.

Keeping my fingers crossed for them, and for Rory.

Friday, March 14, 2008   8:09 p.m.

As I was straightening up the papers on my desk after the last bell today, Lucia stopped by. She seemed a little down, so I invited her to take a seat in the chair next to my desk. She said she had to leave for work soon but agreed to sit for a few minutes. I told her I was glad she came by because I'd been thinking of her.

"How have things been going for you lately?" I ask.

"I haven't missed any of my Language Arts classes," she tells me.

"That's great to hear, Lucia!" I lean over to give her a quick hug.

"Thanks." She smiles but her eyes look tired.

"How's the newborn baby? Still colicky?"

"Yeah, everyone's been up a lot with her during the night trying to help," she answers.

"Boy. That must be rough on everybody."

She nods. "I'm trying as hard as I can to get caught up on my homework Mrs. Mahoney, but it's impossible. There's work, and school, and I'm still tired all the time even if I'm not missing first hour anymore. I'm supposed to be writing a term paper for Language Arts but I haven't been able to come up with my thesis statement yet, and the outline is due the Monday after spring break."

"And you need that class to graduate."

"Yeah. I have to pass that and American Government to get my diploma."

"Would it be possible to take a leave of absence from your job — just until graduation? It would give you a few extra hours every day to get some homework done and maybe even catch up on your rest."

She looks down and silently shakes her head. Her long brown hair hides her face, but I can see the giant teardrops that have fallen onto her faded jeans, leaving two dark blue circles. I grab a Kleenex, hand it to her, and wait until she's ready to talk again.

She wipes her tears away and eventually looks up. "I found out a few days ago my parents haven't paid the rent in two months. We got an eviction notice saying we have to be out of the apartment by the end of the month. I knew money was tight but I never thought we'd get evicted."

She goes on to tell me her aunt and uncle have some friends who will take in the two of them and their baby, and there's a family at church who's offered to take in Lucia's family (mom, dad, Lucia, and her three younger brothers). But that means they'd be moving into a different school district. I don't *think* they'd make Lucia transfer right before graduation, but who knows. And the apartment they'd be moving into is even smaller than the one they're moving out of. What's more, the family they'd be staying with already has two little kids of their own. That makes ten people in one apartment. And the possibility of having to switch high schools.

"I think I'm just going to move in with Brian," Lucia says. "He's been asking me to live with him for a while now anyway."

"Wouldn't that be even more expensive, since you'd have to split the rent and utilities and all that?" I ask.

"If I quit school, I can get more hours at the salon."

"But what about getting your diploma and going to cosmetology school like we talked about?"

"I'm never gonna be able to finish this term paper, so what's the point?"

"Lucia, you only have two more months until graduation. I know that seems a long way off, but in the grand scheme of things it's just a blink of an eye." I want to say more, like how she'd regret it for the rest of her life if she quits school now, but I can see how utterly drained she is so I leave it at that.

She presses her lips together, saying nothing as she glances up at the clock.

"Promise me one thing," I say. "Don't make any big decisions until after spring break. And email your Language Arts teacher tonight after work. Maybe you and Mrs. Callahan can work something out on the due date for the outline. I think she'd be willing to work with you on this."

Lucia reluctantly agrees, probably just to get me to stop talking. "Okay," she says. "But I have to get going. I'm going to be late for work. I just wanted to stop in and say hi." She takes a compact mirror out of her bag and checks her make-up.

I scribble my number on a Post-it and hand it to her. "Here," I say. "This is my cell phone number. You can call me anytime during spring break. Even if you just want to talk. But don't give up on school yet, okay?"

"Okay, thanks." She puts the piece of paper in her purse and heads for the door. Before leaving she stops and turns around. "Do you give your phone number out to everybody? Or is it just me, because I'm special?"

"No, I don't. And yes, you're special."

My reply makes her smile.

After she leaves I make a note to stop by Mrs. Callahan's room on my way out to let her know Lucia might be contacting her. Maybe if Lucia catches up on some sleep over spring break she'll see the wisdom of sticking it out two more months.

Saturday, March 15, 2008   10:50 a.m.

Speaking of spring break, Finn was totally pissed off when he woke up this morning.

I could tell something was bothering him as soon as he came downstairs. I was sitting at the kitchen table, drinking my coffee and doing the crossword puzzle, when he comes in to make himself a bowl of Count Chocula. (I know. You don't like the kids eating that stuff. No one has touched your box of Frosted Mini Wheats since you left. And it'll probably be here waiting for you when you get back.)

I glance up from my crossword and say, "Good morning, sweetheart."

Finn stops dumping cereal into his bowl long enough to look at me as if I'd said "Go fuck yourself" instead of "Good morning."

I continue working on my crossword. "Somebody got up on the wrong side of the bed."

He stomps around the kitchen, slamming cupboards and whatnot, then sits down across from me, shoveling spoonfuls of cereal in his mouth and crunching as loudly as possible.

I continue my crossword and pretend not to notice but I can see him out of the corner of my eye, glaring at me. I think if I just wait long enough, his mood will improve along with the level of geedunk he's putting in his gut. Either that or he'll get tired of scowling and just come out and tell me whatever it was that crawled up his ass and died in the middle of the night.

(By the way, I miss having you around when I'm doing the weekend crossword. I even miss it when I ask you sports questions and you think it's funny to give me a wrong answer that has the same number of letters as the right answer.)

Finn finishes his cereal but continues glowering at me from across the table.

I put down my pen (yes I still do the crossword in pen, no matter how many times you try to mess me up). I fold my hands over the paper and ask, "Is there something on your mind?"

"Oh. Other than the fact that *all* the kids at school yesterday were talking about the big cruise to Mexico, how they're all gonna go drinking in the bars and swim in the ocean and lay on the beach and come back to school next week with suntans? And I'm the only one in the entire senior class staying back here in this shitty little town?"

"Finn. You're not the only senior staying home over spring break. And besides, I thought we settled all this before Dad left?"

"Explain to me again why I couldn't go to Mexico with everyone else?" he says.

"Well, as Dad and I told you back in December, we don't think you're old enough to go on a trip like that. But more importantly, it would be too hard on our budget. With your dad in the military — even on an officer's salary — we can't afford big trips like that every year."

"What about that trip to Hawaii we took two summers ago?" he asks. "That trip cost a lot of money."

"Yes, and we saved up a long time for that," I remind him. "And if you recall, we stayed on the military base instead of in a regular hotel, which saved us a ton of money."

He continues glaring at me but says nothing.

"Finn, even if we could afford a trip to Mexico, it wouldn't be fair to Dad for us to go on a big vacation without him."

"Well why can't Dad have a better job? One where he doesn't have to be gone all the time? Why does he even have to be in the military? Why can't he work at a regular company like all the other dads around here?" Finn gets up from the table and stomps to the kitchen sink where he puts his empty bowl. He stares out the kitchen window, fuming.

I get up and walk over to where he's standing. I want to wrap my arms around him but he's giving off that "don't even think about touching me" vibe so I lean against the counter alongside him. "You're usually so proud of your dad. What's going on?"

"Nothing's 'going on'," he says, using air quotes to punctuate his reply. He turns to look at me. "And why can't you have a better job? Like one that actually uses your degree? Why did you take that stupid ISS job anyway? Why couldn't you be an English teacher or work at some big ad agency like Mrs. Harris?"

I want to tell Finn the reason I don't have a better job is because how can anybody build a career when they have to move every three years? Even if I'd wanted to be a teacher (instead of "just the ISS lady") — I'd have to get licensed all over again every time we moved to a different state. And what company wants to hire somebody who's all but guaranteed to be gone in three years?

But this is not about me, and what's more, I'm beginning to figure out that Finn's feelings of frustration go well beyond the spring break trip. He's worried about Rory getting bullied at school by some stupid asshole, and he's worried about Fakhir and his family. He doesn't talk about it, but I know he misses you like crazy — and worries about you too. It's a lot to carry for a 17-year old.

"Son. I know this is a hard time for you. I know how much you wanted to go on that trip. And I know you're worried about Rory, and Fakhir — and Dad. And that you miss Dad. I miss him too. But we're gonna get through this. And you've got some really exciting things coming up — graduation, and going off to college in the fall. It's gonna be great. And Dad will be back home before you know it."

His shoulders relax the tiniest bit. Once again he says nothing but at least he returns my gaze with something less than hatred.

"What do you say we do some fun things this week?" I offer. "I know Neil's not here but how about Crystal and Darryl? We can invite them over, and Rory can invite Josh, and we'll do some fun stuff together."

Finn looks out the window again. "Are we going to the St. Patrick's parade like we always do?"

"Of course we are. Let's bring your friends and we'll invite everyone to the house for dinner afterward. Why don't you go wake up Rory and you two can start planning everything?"

Liam, I'm in our room now, sitting at my little writing desk by the window, and I can hear Finn and Rory talking in Rory's room, making plans for the week. My first thought was not to tell you about this conversation because I don't want to make you feel bad. But in the end I decided you'd rather know how much you're missed.

Sunday, March 16, 2008   5:19 p.m.

What a wonderful surprise to hear from you last night. I wasn't expecting you to call until today. Everyone was in a great mood after hearing your voice. You made Fakhir's night too when you asked to speak with him for a few minutes.

I'm glad you've been receiving lots of cards and letters from everyone here at home. And who is this new pen pal you have in Los Angeles? Should I be worried? I know you said she's in her seventies, but. …

Also, thanks for looking into what's going on with your paychecks. I'll let you know if the correct amount doesn't show up by next pay period. (The deposit on Friday was still the same wrong amount.)

I was floored when you brought up the idea of inviting Lucia to come live with us for a few months. How did you know I'd been thinking that very same thing? The thought crossed my mind the other night when I wrote to you about her, but I didn't say anything for fear you'd think I had finally gone off the deep end. And then you bring it up on the phone! I'm glad you and I still think alike, even though we're farther apart than ever.

I'll talk it over with Finn and Rory before we make any moves. And I suppose I should talk to the principal to make sure we're not breaking any district rules by having Lucia come live with us. If it means the difference between her being able to graduate or not, I'm sure Dr. Gouwens will be supportive. Once we get the go-ahead from the boys and the school, we'll need to get approval from Lucia's parents. And then from Lucia herself.

Assuming everyone is on board, I was thinking — since Fakhir is already in the guest bedroom in the basement — we could ask Rory to move out of his room and in with Finn. It would only be for a couple months. Of course we'll have to make sure Finn is okay with the arrangement too. If everyone agrees, Lucia could stay in Rory's room.

This could be a great solution for Lucia. She'd have enough peace and quiet to get a good night's sleep, focus on her school work, pass her classes, and get her diploma. Once she has her diploma in hand, she can decide if she wants to apply to cosmetology school or do something different. Either way, she won't have limited her options by not finishing high school.

I'm sure she'll be no trouble at all. Between going to school and working at the salon, it's not like she'll be around all that much. And besides, I wouldn't mind having another girl in the house to balance out all the testosterone flying around here. The only thing I worry about is if Lucia will mind sharing a room with Ozzy and Elvis. Or do you think Rory should move the terrarium and goldfish bowl out of his room and into Finn's room? Nevermind — I'm getting ahead of myself again.

And who knows? It's possible Lucia wouldn't even consider the idea of moving in with this crazy family of ours, even for a short while. I just hope she hasn't already made any big decisions — like quitting school or moving in with her boyfriend — before we have a chance to talk to her.

Monday, March 17, 2008   8:59 p.m.

I don't suppose they served corned beef and cabbage at the DFAC today? The parade this morning was wet and chilly but we had fun in spite of the weather. All seven of us crammed into the car (Finn, Crystal, Darryl, Rory, Josh, Fakhir, and me), and we even got there early enough to get our usual spot near the reviewing stand.

It being Fakhir's first St. Patrick's Day parade, he was somewhat taken aback by the shenanigans going on around us. And I did notice him scanning the crowds and rooftops when we first got there. It wasn't that long ago he left Baghdad — you can't blame the guy for going on high alert in the middle of a raucous crowd.

I put a hand on his shoulder and quietly ask, "You okay?"

"You caught me," he says with a sheepish smile.

"Uh-uh."

"I'll be fine," he reassures me.

I point out all the cops on horseback. "I think we're relatively safe here."

"Got it," he replies. He takes a deep breath, as if willing himself to relax.

"The main thing you're going to have to look out for," I explain, "are the people who've been drinking green beer since they woke up this morning. Stay away from them — you don't want someone puking on your shoes."

I had put the corned beef in the slow cooker before we left, so when we got home the house smelled delicious — especially after we'd been standing outside in the cold all day. I showed Fakhir how to use the potato peeler, then I cut up some carrots and onions while he peeled potatoes. We threw everything into the pot with the beef to simmer some more. When it was almost done I added the cabbage, put out the Irish soda bread I made last night, and called the kids up from the basement where they'd been playing Guitar Hero. Not authentic Irish fare by any stretch (except for the soda bread maybe). But it's our tradition, and we have to keep the traditions going even when you're not here to enjoy them with us.

Fakhir had never eaten corned beef so it was a new experience for him. He tried to be polite about it but I could tell he wasn't too enamored. (I can't say I blame him; it's an acquired taste.) Come to think of it, the boys' friends didn't seem too excited about the corned beef either, but they did get a kick out of the green food coloring I put in their milk. (I couldn't very well serve them green beer now could I?)

The kids cleared the table and did the dishes while I made Irish coffee for Fakhir and me. The main course had failed to win him over, but he did love my Irish coffee. After the kids went outside to shoot hoops on the driveway, he and I sat at the table sipping our coffee and chatting. It was pleasant enough, but my heart ached a little inside. Being with you on St. Paddy's Day, sitting in the kitchen drinking our Irish coffee together, is one of my favorite things in the whole world.

Now I'm snuggled in bed with the pets and my laptop writing you this email. Fakhir has to get up early for work in the morning so he turned in for the night. Finn drove everyone to McDonald's to get shamrock shakes. I'm getting ready to watch John Wayne and Maureen O'Hara in "The Quiet Man" — our final tradition of the day.

Next year this time we'll be together.

Tuesday, March 18, 2008   7:29 p.m.

We loved the video clip you sent of the Royal Tongan Marines doing one of their chants in the palace rotunda. What an experience it must have been to see and hear them in person! Now that I've seen the video I can understand how motivating it is to hear them shout "Oorah!" whenever a Marine walks through a checkpoint.

After I saw your clip I went online to find out more. I came across an article that said Tonga is a small island between Australia and Tahiti. (I had never even heard of it before.) It also said Tongans fought alongside Marines at the Battle of Guadalcanal during WWII. Another article said there's 55 Tongans in each contingent sent to Iraq to serve as a security force for the MNC command center in Al Faw Palace. That's you right?

I stopped reading when the article mentioned the palace as an inviting target for insurgents. Sometimes my curiosity gets the best of me.

All is well here. It's a wonderful feeling to be caught up on housework, laundry, and bills. I even had some time to work on our budget. Once your paychecks get squared away, we may have a little left over each month to put into savings. With what I make from my job, maybe we can take the kids on a little vacation after you get back.

Other than the rocky start with Finn at the beginning of the break, we've had a relaxing week so far. (Well, all of us except for Fakhir, who's still working extra hours.) After I finish writing you this email I'm going to get back to reading Candice Millard's *River of Doubt*. It's as good as you said it was — thanks for recommending it. (And I already finished our book club selection for this month so your timing was perfect.)

Finn went with Crystal and Darryl to a café downtown that's supposedly a hookah bar. I wasn't going to let him go but I've been feeling a little guilty about not letting him go to Mexico (I know, I know), which led me to say yes to the hookah bar against my better judgment. I suppose he could have gone anyway without telling me, so I'm glad he was at least honest enough to ask me in the first place.

Even though they spend a ton of time together I've come to believe Finn and Crystal really are just friends. Maybe they had a brief fling around the time of the Turnabout Dance (and that time she left her sweater here — cough cough), but I get the sense they're more like best buddies now. I do think Rory has developed something of a crush on Crystal (beginning with the time he saw her wearing nothing but blue-tinted plastic wrap). When we were walking from the parade back to the car yesterday I noticed Rory walked behind Crystal the whole time so he could watch her butt. And then when everyone piled in the car to go home he told her she could sit on his lap. Which she did. I could see Rory's face in the rearview mirror and he couldn't stop grinning the entire ride home. At least he's gotten over Ashley. I hear she's dating someone on the soccer team now.

Josh's mom took Rory and Josh and some other boys to play paintball today. There again it was a little more expensive than what I'd normally allow Rory to spend, but I thought it would be good for him to do something special this week too. I haven't let him hang out at Jack in the Box since the beer debacle with Ethan last month. Come to think of it, Rory hasn't seen Ethan around much lately.

Wednesday, March 19, 2008   9:17 p.m.

Oh God. Just when we start to relax something bad happens. Fakhir spoke to his mother this morning before work. Fakhir's youngest sister (Farah) found the family dog in the back yard with its throat slit.

Fakhir immediately called his boss to tell him he'd be late for work. Then he called his uncle (not the one who lives in Norway — the one who lives in Iraq, somewhere outside of Baghdad) to ask if his mother and sisters can come live with him and his family until their visas get approved. Fakhir thinks that if his family can be moved without the insurgents knowing, they'll be safe for a while. Obviously it would be a tricky operation, since they now realize the insurgents must be watching the house. I thought the guys from Camp Slayer were watching the house too, but somehow one of those jackass prickfucks managed to slip past them and into the back yard undetected. The insurgents probably waited until Fakhir's mom and sisters were asleep, then created some sort of distraction to get past our surveillance team.

After Fakhir got off the phone with his uncle (who of course said yes) he called Maj. Salazar. Ray was at work and therefore able to patch a call through the DSN line right away to talk with the team at Camp Slayer (they were already aware of the situation). I guess all this circuitous calling is to prevent classified info from being discussed on the family's personal phones, which everyone now assumes are being monitored. The intel team gets messages containing sensitive information to the family by sending guys from the Iraqi security force to the house disguised as government employees coming to check on the electricity or as a neighborhood merchant pushing a fruit cart or something. (It just occurred to me — do you already know all this?)

Fakhir ended up staying at the house all morning waiting for a callback from Ray, who eventually called a couple hours later. He told Fakhir our guys at Camp Slayer were able to communicate with Fakhir's uncle outside of Baghdad, and the plan now is to transport Fakhir's family via some sort of undercover means as soon as they determine it's safe to move them. Someone will get a message to Fakhir's mom and sisters to start packing their belongings into two suitcases each, in the likely event they'll have to leave on short notice. Can you imagine having to sort through a lifetime's worth of possessions, keeping only what you can carry in two suitcases?

Everyone is heartbroken about the dog, including Fakhir. That was the pet he was talking about when he told me his family had a dog but it was an outside dog. They've had her since Fakhir was 12, and he's 27 now, so the dog would have been 15. But Fakhir said she still had the energy of a pup last time he saw her, which was right before he left for the U.S. in December.

All this happened before the boys had even gotten out of bed (I've been letting them sleep til noon, and yes I know you find that appalling). Fakhir and I talked it over and we decided we weren't going to tell Finn and Rory about the dog. It's not something they need to know, and we don't want to put a cloud over their spring break.

I hope Fakhir's family can be moved to safety before something worse happens.

Coming Soon:

Since You Went Away, Part Two: Spring

Glossary

I MEF: 1st Marine Expeditionary Force, or "One MEF." A Marine Air Ground Task Force (MAGTF) based out of Marine Corps Base Camp Pendleton and the largest of the three MEFs in the Fleet Marine Force.

3rd MAW: 3rd Marine Aircraft Wing. Provides the aviation combat element for I MEF (see above), based out of Marine Corps Air Station Miramar.

AAR: After Action Report. A tool used by all military branches for either formally or informally evaluating a particular event after it occurs.

ABC party: Anything But Clothes party in which attendees wear non-traditional, non-fabric materials.

and a wake-up: used when counting down the days to an anticipated event. For example, "four days and a wake-up" equals five days.

AWOL: Absent Without Official Leave.

Basic School (TBS): The Basic School, in Quantico Virginia, a six-month program in which all newly commissioned U.S. Marine Corps officers further develop their leadership skills.

battalion: In the Marine Corps, a unit composed of a headquarters and two or more companies with a total of 500 to 1,200 Marines.

BCGs: Boot Camp Glasses, issued to Marines at boot camp. Also known as Birth Control Glasses because, well, take a look at someone who's wearing a pair.

BGen: Brigadier General (0-7).

blue falcon: Buddy Fucker. Someone who puts himself (or herself) first at the expense of his (or her) fellow service members.

blue star: Traditionally, a blue star on a service flag indicates an active-duty family member has been deployed to a combat zone during a time of war or hostilities. More recently (in the years following the time period depicted in this novel), the meaning of the blue star has been widened to include those serving during a time of war (not necessarily deployed to a combat zone). The service flag is typically hung facing out from the inside of a front window of the home where the service member normally resides.

Bravo Zulu: well done.

brig: a jail on a naval vessel. Usage later expanded to mean any jail or prison on a military installation.

brigade: In the Marine Corps, a formation that consists of a minimum of three regimental-equivalent sized units.

Bronze Star: Officially known as the Bronze Star Medal, awarded to members of the U.S. Armed Forces (as well as civilians serving with military forces in combat) for heroic achievement, heroic service, meritorious achievement, or meritorious service in a combat zone.

BTW: by the way

butthurt: annoyed, upset, or angry about something others perceive as trivial.

CACO: Casualty Assistance Calls Officer. A member of a two- or three-person team consisting of a notifications officer, casualty assistance officer, and chaplain whose job is to provide in-person notification and support to next of kin when a service member has died.

cammies: camouflage utility uniform.

Camp Slayer: a former Iraqi government palace complex located on the southeastern corner of the Baghdad International Airport, used as a U.S. military base during the Iraq war.

casualty officer: see CACO.

CHAOS: Colonel Has Another Outstanding Suggestion.

Charlies: Marine Corps service uniform consisting of green trousers (or skirt) and khaki shirt. Variations of this uniform are known as Alpha (Service "A" uniform worn with green coat), Bravo (Service "B" uniform with no coat and long-sleeve shirt), and Charlie (Service "C" uniform with no coat and short-sleeve shirt).

Chesty: The English bulldog mascot of the Marine Corps, named after Lt.Gen. Lewis B. "Chesty" Puller Jr., one of the most decorated Marines in history.

chow hall: cafeteria in a military installation, also known as a mess hall or DFAC.

CHU: Containerized Housing Unit, a pre-fabricated shipping container used as temporary living quarters on military installations.

CO: Commanding Officer.

Col.: Colonel (O-6).

combat pay: service members assigned to a combat zone receive combat pay, officially known as Imminent Danger Pay (IDP).

command: a body of troops or a station, ship, etc. under the leadership of an officer.

commissary: grocery store on a military base.

Cpl.: Corporal (E-4).

CTU: Counter Terrorism Unit (as referred to in the TV show "24").

DD: Designated Driver.

deployment: the temporary relocation of armed forces and materiel within operational areas.

Deployment Curse: Murphy's Law for military spouses. Things tend to go wrong (appliances break, kids get sick, car battery dies) with greater frequency as soon as the service member leaves on a deployment.

Deployment Perk: Privileges or benefits given to family members in an effort to lighten the load for the military family when their service member is deployed. Can include discounts on goods and services or babysitting, meals, transportation, and cards proffered by friends and neighbors.

DFAC: (pronounced *dee-fack*) Dining Facility.

DFAS: Defense Finance and Accounting Service.

DHARMA Initiative: Department of Heuristics and Research on Material Applications, a fictional research project featured on the television series "Lost."

dilliclapper: Do I Look Like I Could Lead A Platoon?, a person who does not make good decisions.

DoD: Department of Defense.

douchenozzle: a person who acts like a jackass, more so than a douchebag.

DSN: Defense Switched Network. Department of Defense telecommunications system used for official business.

ducks in a row: To organize and take care of details before beginning a project. Origin uncertain. Could be a Navy shipbuilding term wherein the heaviest parts of the ship are lined up before being lifted by a crane. Or a reference to the energy-efficient V-formation of ducks in flight. Or the way baby ducks line up behind their mother. Or the line of mechanical ducks at a shooting arcade. Take your pick.

duty station: military base where a service member has been assigned to work as a result of a PCS order.

embrace the suck: To adopt a mindset of not letting unpleasant circumstances determine your attitude. In other words, "The situation is bad, deal with it."

FAFSA: Free Application for Federal Student Aid. The form college students must fill out to be considered for financial aid, student loans, work-study programs, grants, and some scholarships.

FEN: Far East Network. The American military network of radio and television stations that operated primarily in mainland Japan, Okinawa, the Philippines, and Guam until 1997. Now known as AFN (American Forces Network).

flash-blasted: The act of being chewed out by the senior non-commissioned officer (NCO).

FNG: Fucking New Guy.

FOB: Forward Operating Base.

Fobbit: A perjorative used by troops in the field to describe military personnel who spend the majority of their time within the relative safety of the Forwarding Operating Base (FOB).

FRG: Family Readiness Group.

FSG: Family Support Group.

Fuckin' A: Indicates emphatic agreement. The exact origin of this phrase is unknown, but the earliest written records suggest it was used in the 1940s by U.S. service members during WWII. The "A" possibly stands for the aviation term "affirmative" or it may instead refer to "able," the first letter in the military radio alphabet used in WWII.

full battle rattle: protective gear worn by military personnel to include flak jacket, Kevlar helmet, weapon(s), and ammo.

FYSA: For Your Situational Awareness (military version of FYI).

geedunk: snack bar on a ship that sells candy & other junk food, also used to refer to such snacks.

geo-bachelor: geographic bachelor. A common practice for military families in which the military service member lives alone at a duty station while the rest of the family remains in place at another location.

G.I.: a slang term for a service member. Originally an initialism for galvanized iron; later came into widespread use around WWII as an acronym for Government Issue or General Issue.

gold star: a gold star on a service flag indicates a member of one's family was killed while serving in the armed forces during a time of war or hostilities. The service flag is typically hung facing out from the inside of a front window of the home where the service member lived.

gouge: informal but essential information, the facts behind the rumors. Originally a Navy term used in reference to test answers (aka cheat sheet).

Green Zone: heavily fortified headquarters of the Coalition Forces during the Iraq War, now known as the International Zone.

Gunny (GySgt.): Gunnery sergeant (E-7).

gyrene: slang for a U.S. Marine. Origin unknown, though some sources say it's a combination of G.I. and Marine. Commonly used by members of the U.S. Navy during WWI to insult Marines, it instead became a popular way for Marines to refer to one another.

Haji: an honorific title given to a Muslim who has completed the Haji to Mecca; when used by non-Muslims (including American military personnel) it's often a derogatory way of referring to anyone who appears to be a Muslim (whether or not they actually are).

hayaku: Japanese for "faster," frequently used to encourage someone to go faster or hurry up, but also used by American military personnel to mean "leave in a hurry."

head: restroom.

heads-up: an alert or warning.

helot: a member of a class of serfs in ancient Sparta, someone whose social status is between a slave and a citizen. In the movie Meet John Doe, Walter Brennan's character (the Colonel) uses the term helots to describe people who only want something from you ("a lotta heels").

high and tight: a military regulation haircut favored by Marines in which the sides and back are closely shaved (0 inches), with a very gradual and slight increase in length toward the top, usually no more than 1-2 inches (the shorter the better).

HMFIC: Head Mother Fucker In Charge.

Holy Mike Foxtrot: Holy Mother Fucker.

hurt locker: To be in trouble, at a disadvantage, or in bad shape. The term is from the Vietnam era and refers to a situation or mental state, similar to being "in a world of hurt."

HQ: Headquarters.

ICAO: (pronounced eye-kay-oh). International Civil Aviation Organization. The ICAO alphabet is a series of acrophonic codewords assigned to the 26 letters of the English alphabet for use in radio communications. A = Alpha, B = Bravo, C = Charlie, and so on.

IDP: Imminent Danger Pay, also known as combat pay for service members assigned to a combat zone.

IED: Improvised Explosive Device.

IM: Instant Message. A type of Internet-based communication that allows two people to exchange private text-based messages typed in real-time. Also used as a verb to describe the act of exchanging instant messages.

in-country: being in a country for the purpose of military operations.

Insha'Allah: Arabic for "God willing."

intel: short for intelligence. The collection and assessment of data from a range of sources in support of a military command.

International Zone (IZ): formerly known as the Green Zone, the heavily fortified headquarters for the Iraqi Reconstruction Ministries.

invi-told: an invitation to a military event in which attendance is said to be voluntary yet implicitly required in order to remain in good standing.

ISS: In-School Suspension.

IUD: Intrauterine Device. A form of birth control.

jarhead: slang for a U.S. Marine. Ostensibly derived from the similarity in appearance of a Marine in his dress blue uniform (with its stiff, high collar) and a Mason jar. Commonly used by members of the U.S. Navy during WWII to insult Marines, it instead became a popular way for Marines to refer to one another.

JJ DID TIE BUCKLE: The 14 Marine Corps leadership traits: Justice, Judgment, Decisiveness, Initiative, Dependability, Tact, Integrity, Enthusiasm, Bearing, Unselfishness, Courage, Knowledge, Loyalty, Endurance.

Ka-Bar: Combat (or Fighting Utility) knife, first used by the Marine Corps in November 1942 during WWII.

Lima Charlie: loud and clear.

LCpl: Lance Corporal (E-3).

LCpl. Schmuckatelli: A generic term used to describe any hapless Marine who frequently finds himself in trouble and therefore used as an example of what not to do.

Maine Troop Greeters: A volunteer group of veterans and other citizens who greet the troops every time a military flight stops at Bangor International Airport on its way to or from a war zone.

Maj.: Major (O-4).

Maj. Bagadonuts: The officer version of LCpl. Schmuckatelli. A fictional Marine often used as an example of what not to do. A derogatory nickname for an officer on weight control or who has an otherwise subpar appearance.

make a hole: get out of the way.

mandatory fun: a family-oriented military event intended to raise morale but which feels more like an obligation.

MCSF: Marine Corps Support Facility, a Marine Corps base located in New Orleans, LA.

military brat: A term of affection and respect when used by military families. Not recommended for use by people outside the military, as it can be interpreted as being derogatory.

milspouse: Short for military spouse. Other abbreviations include milspo and milso (military significant other).

Mike Foxtrot: Mother Fucker, as in motherfucker.

MIP: Minor In Possession (of alcohol or other illegal substance).

MNC: Multi-National Corps. A multi-national command charged with directing the tactical battle in Iraq under the parent command of Multi-National Force (MNF) which handles strategic level issues.

MNC-I: Multi-National Corps – Iraq. The tactical unit responsible for command and control of operations in Iraq (see MNC above).

MNF: Multi-National Force. The parent command of MNC that handles strategic level issues.

MNF-I: Multi-National Force – Iraq (see MNF above).

moonbeam: flashlight.

mortar: a short-range, short-barrel, muzzle-loading cannon for firing low-speed, high-arcing projectiles at (often unseen) targets.

most ricky-tick: as quickly as possible (see "ricky-tick").

MP: Military Police.

MRE: Meal Ready to Eat. Individual meals used in the field, formerly known as C-Rations or C-Rats.

MUSADI: Makin' Up Shit And Defending It. This is not a documented military acronym but a McCarthy family favorite thanks to Lt.Col. Rich Haddad (USMC Ret.).

MWR: Morale, Welfare & Recreation. A program/facility on military bases that offers recreational activities, discounts, and other services for military members and their families aimed at improving morale.

NCO: Non-Commissioned Officer.

NLT: No Later Than.

no go: not going to happen or do not go.

NOLA: New Orleans.

O Club: Officers' Club. A facility for dining and socializing limited to military officers, their families, and guests.

OCS: Officer Candidate School, a training and screening program for potential Marine Officers.

oddy-knocky: on one's own, alone. A term used by the characters in A Clockwork Orange by Anthony Burgess.

OEF: Operation Enduring Freedom (Afghanistan).

OFP: Own Fucking Program. A Marine not following orders or adhering to Marine Corps standards.

OIF: Operation Iraqi Freedom.

One Mef: phonetic pronunciation of I MEF (1st Marine Expeditionary Force).

Oorah: an expression of enthusiasm specific to the Marine Corps. (Hooah is Army while hooyah is Navy and Coast Guard.)

OPSEC: Operations Security. The practice of controlling the release of unclassified information that, when pieced together with other data, could provide details of military operations to potential adversaries.

Ops O: Operations Officer.

order(s): In the military, an authoritative directive, instruction, or notice issued by a commander or commanding organization.

Oscar Kilo: OK.

OSS: Out-of-School Suspension.

OWC: Officers' Wives Club.

P-38: a small can opener used to open canned field rations, also known as a "John Wayne" by Marines.

paracord bracelet: a survival bracelet made using 550-lb. strength parachute cord (aka 550 cord) that can be unraveled and used in an emergency.

PBJ: If you're an English speaker who had to look this up in the glossary you do not belong on this planet.

PCS: Permanent Change of Station. Frequently used as a verb among military people to describe moving from one duty station to another (as in "we're PCSing next month").

PERSEC: Personal Security. The practice of controlling personal information in order to protect the safety of service members and their families.

PFC: Private First Class (E-2).

PFT: Physical Fitness Test.

pie-hole: mouth.

POG: Persons Other than Grunt. Any non-infantry military personnel. Depending on speaker and context, can be interpreted as either endearing or derogatory.

pop-flare: a hand-held, hand-launched aerial illumination projectile.

pop smoke: to leave in a hurry. Derived from the military practice of either 1.) igniting a smoke grenade so you can make an exit without being detected by the enemy or 2.) marking your landing zone for an aircraft coming to extract you from a bad situation.

pound sand: when used in the imperative, a vehement dismissal (as in "go pound sand").

POV: Point of View, most often used in a literary context to describe who is narrating a story.

PT: Physical Training.

PTSD: Post-Traumatic Stress Disorder.

qadi: Muslim judge.

rack: bed, short for barrack.

rank-dropping: akin to name-dropping, mentioning someone's rank for the sole purpose of impressing others.

recon: short for reconnaissance — to surreptitiously patrol in an effort to gain information.

Ret.: Retired.

Rhino Runner: an armored bus used extensively in Iraq, especially on Route Irish (between Baghdad International Airport and the International Zone).

ricky-tick (also "most ricky-tick"): as soon as possible, quickly. Used by Marines when an order needs to be carried out expeditiously. The origin of this phrase is disputed as either being derived from an unknown Japanese phrase or from the children's tale Rikki Tikki Tavi, in which the title character is a mongoose (known to be extremely fast).

RPG: Ruchnoy Protivotankovy Granatomyot, aka Rocket Propelled Grenade, a hand-held anti-tank grenade launcher.

SACO: Substance Abuse Control Officer.

sandbox: Iraq.

Schmuckatelli: aka LCpl. Schmuckatelli. A generic term used to describe any hapless Marine who frequently finds himself in trouble and therefore used as an example of what not to do.

seabag: cylindrical canvas bag used by sailors and Marines to carry personal items such as uniforms.

sent to the brig: confined to jail on a military installation.

separate: (verb) in the military, when the required term of service has been completed and a service member is released from active duty.

shitbird: A Marine (or anyone) who is not squared away in appearance or discipline.

shithot: A Marine who is tactically skilled, hardcore, way above average. Also applies to an operation that is particularly well carried-out.

shit on a shingle (SOS): creamed chipped beef (or ground beef) on toast, traditionally served in military mess halls.

shitstorm: an extremely unpleasant culmination of unfortunate events.

Sierra Bravo: Shit Bird, as in shitbird.

Sierra Tango Foxtrot Uniform: Shut The Fuck Up.

silkies: Marine Corps PT gear often used for running and/or as underwear. These extremely short, green "silk" shorts were phased out in 2011 in spite of a cult following among Marines (and their admirers).

sit rep: situational report.

Skype: a software application that allows people to talk in real-time using their computers and an Internet connection, usually via video. Also used as a verb to describe the act of video chatting.

smoking lamp: a nautical term used to signify when smoking is allowed on a ship; when the smoking lamp is lighted, smoking is allowed; when the smoking lamp is out, smoking is not allowed.

SNL: Saturday Night Live.

SOL: Shit Outta Luck.

SOS: Shit On a Shingle (chipped beef on toast).

soup sandwich: messy situation.

spousal unit: Military wife or husband, suggesting she/he was issued to the service member similar to other military gear. Can be used affectionately or not.

squared away: A nautical term meaning to align the sails at right angles to the mast and keel of a ship for optimal wind direction. In general military terms, to be organized and ready.

SRO: School Resource Officer. A police officer responsible for providing law enforcement and crime prevention in the public school environment.

SSgt: Staff Sergeant (E-6).

stay frosty: be alert and on guard.

stealth wife: A stealth wife (or husband) is a military spouse whose efforts are often invisible but who supports the mission by working behind the scenes to keep the family and household running smoothly, especially during deployments.

TAD: Temporary Assigned Duty. A Navy and Marine Corps term for a service member's travel assignment to a location other than one's permanent duty station. Also known as TDY (Temporary Duty) among other service branches as well as the general military population.

Tango Yankee: Thank You.

tasker: an official DoD document that contains a direction to perform specific tasks. Informally, another thing to do in addition to all the other things a person has to do.

T-minus: In aeronautical terms, the time before rocket launch. In military circles, commonly used to refer to the time until a service member returns home after a deployment, used for countdown purposes.

TBS: The Basic School, in Quantico Virginia, a six-month program in which all newly commissioned U.S. Marine Corps officers further develop their leadership skills.

TDY: Temporary Duty. Also known as TAD (Temporary Additional Duty) in the Navy and Marine Corps. Refers to a service member's travel assignment to a location other than one's permanent duty station.

terp: short for interpreter.

thousand-yard stare: a vacant or unfocused gaze into the distance exhibited by war-weary service members.

TK: short for "to come," a publishing reference used as a placeholder for an item yet to be inserted.

TMI: Too Much Information.

tour: period of military service in one location.

un-ass: to leave the area, remove one's butt from wherever it happens to be resting.

un-fuck: to correct a deficiency, usually on a person, to bring something or someone into proper order.

unsat: unsatisfactory. A behavior that is well below the required standards.

USO: United Service Organizations, a non-profit group that provides programs and services to military members and their families.

VA: Veterans Affairs.

VBC: Victory Base Complex (Iraq). A cluster of military installations to include Camp Victory, where Al-Faw Palace was located and which housed the headquarters of the Multi-National Corps — Iraq (MNC I).

visual contact: sighting of a friendly aircraft/ground position.

voluntold: When a service member (or family member) is encouraged to participate in an activity that appears voluntary but in reality is not voluntary at all.

VTC: Video Teleconference.

War Department: a service member's spouse. Can be used affectionately or not.

wheels up: ready for departure.

Whiskey Delta: Weak Dick.

Whiskey Tango Foxtrot: What The Fuck.

Wilco: Will comply, meaning "I understand and will do as instructed."

XO: Executive Officer. The second in command of a unit under the CO (Commanding Officer).

Author's Note

Although this is a work of fiction, real-world historic and cultural events appear throughout the story. While I've tried as much as possible to incorporate these events accurately and in the correct timeframe in which they occurred, some events have been reworked to fit the narrative. For example:

Books, movies, & other media

Emilie mentions reading David Sedaris' *When You Are Engulfed In Flames* in February 2008, but the book wasn't released until June 2008. Likewise, although she mentions her book club reading Dave Cullen's *Columbine* in March 2008, that book didn't come out until a year later, in 2009. She also mentions "the new Shrek movie" in February 2008, which came out in May 2007. Most of the classic movies referenced in the story were aired on Turner Classic Movies, though not necessarily on the dates mentioned. Emilie's book club read *Still Alice* in May 2008, yet although author Lisa Genova self-published the book in 2007, *Still Alice* wasn't in wide distribution until January 2009. Ethan mentions playing "the new Call of Duty game" in May 2008, although Call of Duty wasn't released until November of that year. Lindsay Shannon's blues program on KCFX runs from 8-10 p.m. on Sunday nights even though Emilie and Wade listen to it in the car on a Saturday afternoon.

News/historic events

Although the Virginia Tech massacre occurred on April 16, 2007, it was mentioned here as having happened one year later (April 16, 2008). And while several U.S. colonels were killed during Operation Iraqi Freedom, all news items that appear in this story are entirely fictitious, as are all other events involving the fictional characters in this book. For example, although the Mahdi Army was involved in acts of violence against Coalition forces in Ramadi, Sadr City, and elsewhere in 2008, the incident described by Fakhir is entirely fictional. Emilie references the Military Spouse of the Year Award as if it's been in existence a while, even though the award was first given in 2008. In an email from April 2008 Emilie mentions burn pits even though the use of burn pits in Iraq and Afghanistan wasn't in the news or widely known until several months later. The Veterans Crisis Line was launched in 2007 but until 2011 it was called the National Veterans Suicide Prevention Hotline — hence, certain characters in this story don't consider calling the Hotline in 2008 for non-suicide-related assistance.

Pop culture & miscellaneous other stuff

Will Ferrell's "The Luxury Spy" Jaguar skit didn't happen until 2010 even though Emilie references it in a June 2008 email. Emilie is mentioned drinking Boulevard Brewery's Tank 7 Farmhouse Ale in 2008 even though that particular beer didn't make its debut until 2009. Aunt Dottie mentions Katy Perry's hair being blue and purple in 2008 even though Perry didn't start using those hues until a couple years later. Emilie uses the phrase "sorry not sorry," which didn't come into popular use until 2011.

A note on becoming a U.S. citizen

U.S. Citizenship and Immigration Services requires most immigrants to live in the U.S. five years before they can apply for citizenship; there is an exemption from this requirement, however, for those who served in the U.S. military for at least a year and who are applying for citizenship within six months of an honorable discharge. The fictional portrayal of

Fakhir's naturalization process was sped up to fit the narrative and does not reflect the actual time required to become a U.S. citizen. Also, while Fakhir's backstory is that he came to the U.S. on a Special Immigrant Visa for interpreters in late 2007, that program wasn't instituted until 2008, when it was passed into law as part of the National Defense Authorization Act of 2008.

A note on style

Traditionally, the term "Marine" (when referring to individual members of the U.S. Marine Corps) wasn't capitalized until recent years, when news outlets such as the Associated Press, The New York Times, and the Chicago Tribune began capitalizing it. I use the modern, capitalized version of "Marine" in keeping with these recent changes.

Acknowledgments

With gratitude to:

Margaret Buell Wilder, author of the original *Since You Went Away ... Letters to a Soldier from His Wife* (Whittlesey House, 1943) and David O. Selznick, producer and co-screenwriter (with Wilder) of the 1944 movie adaptation of the book (also named *Since You Went Away*). Both served as inspiration for this modern-day story.

Mustafa and Asad, friends and Marine Corps combat interpreters, for sharing their stories.

Anne Stroh, who connected with my husband via Operation Paperback during his tour in Iraq and became a close friend of our family. An astute reader and witty conversationalist, Anne edited this manuscript as it was being written — offering just the right amount of gentle prodding, constructive criticism, and reassuring repartee every step of the way.

Carolyn Graan, longtime friend and early reader who helped me find my voice.

Gerarda Simmons, Patricia McCarthy, and Roger Laven, for their encouragement.

Dr. Amy Murphy, for answering my questions about high school administration. Sahar Chapuk, for answering my random questions about language & culture in Iraq.

David High of High Design for his marvelous cover designs.

Kevin Callahan of BNGO Books for his equally marvelous production work on both ebook & print versions.

Kevin Callahan and David High for their collaboration on a thoughtful & lovely interior design.

Faith Simmons for her perspicacious copyediting. (Did I spell that right?)

David Blatner, for his magical technical expertise in all things digital prepress.

The members of Paperback Readers Book Club, who uplifted me during Pat's deployment and continue to uplift with their wit and laughter.

My husband Pat, whose military service not only shaped this story but shaped who we are as a family. Pat also served as my sounding board when I was stuck and my on-site consultant when I had military-related questions. (Any errors — military or otherwise — are my own.)

Our sons Ben and Coleman, who didn't ask to be born into a military family but who served nonetheless.

The Marines of Marine Corps Mobilization Command/Marine Corps Reserve Support Command, for watching over us while Pat was deployed, especially Maj. John Whyte.

All members of the military, past and present, who dedicate their lives to serving others, and to their families, who keep watch and wait.

About the Author

Nan McCarthy is the author of *Since You Went Away, Chat, Connect, & Crash, Live 'Til I Die,* and *Quark Design.* The *Chat, Connect & Crash* series, originally self-published, was acquired by Simon & Schuster and published in trade paperback in 1998. Nan regained the rights to the series and released new editions in 2014. A former magazine editor & technology writer, Nan founded Rainwater Press in 1992 and began selling her books online in 1995. Nan and her husband, a veteran who served 29 years in the Marine Corps, are the proud parents of two adult sons. Nan wrote *Since You Went Away* after taking a ten-year break from full-time writing to care for the family during her husband's frequent military travels.

10% of the net profits from the sale of digital and printed copies of *Since You Went Away, Part One: Winter* will be donated to the Semper Fi Fund. The Semper Fi Fund provides immediate and long-term support for post-9/11 injured and critically ill members of all branches of the U.S. Armed Forces and their families, including direct financial assistance, career transition assistance, specialized support for service members who suffer from PTSD and TBI, grants for therapeutic arts, and the Veteran 2 Veteran (V2V) program which trains and empowers veterans to help other veterans make a successful transition to civilian life. The Semper Fi Fund was founded in 2004 by a group of Marine Corps spouses.

Also by Nan McCarthy

Fiction
Chat: Book One
Connect: Book Two
Crash: Book Three

Non-fiction
Live 'Til I Die
Quark Design

You can find Nan online in the following places:

nan-mccarthy.com

facebook.com/nanmccarthywriter

instagram.com/nanmccarthy

twitter.com/nanmccarthy

pinterest.com/nanmccarthy

To reach Nan directly, please use the Contact form on her website: nan-mccarthy.com/contact/

Veterans Crisis Line: Call (800) 273-8255 and press "1" to talk to someone right away. Text 838255 from your mobile phone. Or go online at
www.veteranscrisisline.net and click "Confidential Veterans Chat."